# Jewish Sci-Fi Stories

# for Kids

# Jewish Sci-fi Stories for Kids

PITSPOPANY

New York & Jerusalem

Published by Pitspopany Press Copyright ©1999

Cover Design by Ben Gasner
Book Design by Sourcegrafix
Illustrations by Rivka Lisa Perel

Cloth   ISBN: 0-943706-73-4
Paper   ISBN: 0-943706-74-2

Pitspopany Press titles may be purchased for fund-raising programs by schools and organizations by contacting:

Marketing Director, Pitspopany Press
40 East 78th Street, Suite 16D
New York, New York 10021
Tel: (800) 232-2931
Fax: (212) 472-6253
Email: pop@netvision.net.il

Printed in Hungary

To the birth of a new genre!

JEWISH SCIENCE FICTION


*And why not?*

# TABLE OF CONTENTS

# Breath of Clay

by Stephanie Burgis

STEPHANIE BURGIS is a member of the Clarion Science Fiction and Fantasy Writer's Workshop in East Lansing, Michigan. She is also a Fulbright Scholar, a music history scholar, and musician.

After visiting Prague, Stephanie felt the need to write the story you are about to read. She's not alone. There are over a dozen variations of this story.

But none quite like this....

During the spring that Jakob turned eleven years old, the emperor's soldiers filled the streets of Prague with shining boots and helmets and swords that flashed brightly in the sun. While the rest of the Jewish families in Jakob's neighborhood filled window boxes with flowers and began spring cleaning, Jakob collected rent on the first Tuesday of every month. He held the money pouch carefully as he trudged up the stairs, and tried very hard not to think about the vast pool of silence collecting below him, where his mother lay in their apartment, staring into an unimaginable distance.

Wisps of smoke and the unmistakable scent of incense beckoned him upwards, towards the attic, but he stopped first on the second floor.

"What, it's time to steal my money again? Thieves!" The deep baritone voice bellowed through the door, filling the hallway. "Come in, come in! Fool that I am, I don't lock my door."

Jakob pinned a determined, polite smile on his face and opened the door.

"Good morning, Herr Goldberg."

The vast mass in the chair snorted. "A fine

morning, Jakob. Here to steal my hard-earned money, as if the taxes didn't take enough." He sighed, and then laughed as he saw Jakob's face. "I don't bite, boy! It's only a little complaining, which I deserve at my age. Come here, come here. How much is it this month?"

"The same as always, Herr Goldberg." Jakob held out the bag.

"Ah. Sweet continuity." Goldberg reached into his desk drawer, and counted out gulden. "Here you are. And a little extra for a newspaper—and even more for a candy, for being so patient with an old man."

Jakob drew the bag closed. "Thank you, sir. I'll bring you the newspaper this afternoon."

He turned to leave, but Goldberg's voice forestalled him. "So, Jakob. So." The humor left his face, as his thick eyebrows lowered. "You are our rent collector again this month. Does your mother still refuse to face the world?"

Jakob felt his face stiffen. "My mother...is perfectly well, Herr Goldberg, sir. There is nothing wrong."

*She won't talk. She won't even look at me. I don't think she even remembers that she has a son.*

"There is nothing wrong," Jakob repeated. His voice sounded tinny in his own ears, and very faint.

"Hum." Goldberg studied him for a moment longer. "And what do you do with yourself, when you aren't collecting rent for your mother? You're a young boy, you must want to do something for yourself, for amusement."

Jakob swallowed. "I go with Frau Schuman and her daughters to synagogue, sir. And I run chores for them, when they need me." Suddenly remembering, his face lit up. "And I go to see the soldiers, too! They have big long swords, sir, and such beautiful uniforms, I think—"

"Hush!" Goldberg's voice was suddenly harsh. "Don't talk about that, Jakob! You—you have better things to do. And your mother needs you at home, to help, I'm sure."

Jakob frowned. "But sir, I—"

Goldberg sighed. "Never mind. I know you don't mean—you don't know.... At any rate, good luck to you, my boy. And be fast about that newspaper! I have little enough else to occupy me, these days."

"Yes, sir." Relieved, Jakob escaped.

The incense was stronger now, filling his nose and making him dizzy as he climbed up the curving staircase to the attic. As he raised his hand to knock on the door, he heard slow words, in a voice so changed that he hardly recognized it. They cut off abruptly when the knocks sounded. Jakob heard rustling, and quick movement. A minute later, a voice answered him.

"Come in!"

As Jakob opened the door, he jumped back in surprise. A cat—was it a cat? He had never seen one of that color before—raced towards him and then, disconcertingly, slipped through his leg with a feeling like ice, and became a cloud of blue smoke, floating behind him. It vanished with a soft pop, and Jakob, swallowing hard, looked up. His mother's second tenant slammed the top drawer of his writing desk shut and jumped back with a fixed smile. He pushed his glasses up higher on his long nose, and ran a trembling hand through his thin hair.

"Yes? Can I help you with something, Jakob?"

Jakob pointed behind him, to where the cloud of smoke had hung.

"Herr Koenig, what was that?"

"What? I didn't see anything."

"There was—it looked like—"

"Oh, I know why you're here. It's time to pay rent, isn't it? Let me find my money. Your mother—such a charming lady—very understanding—let me look...." Koenig walked hastily over to the overflowing bookcase and picked out a thick, handsomely bound book. He flipped through the pages. "I thought I put it...."

Jakob stepped up behind him, trying to look over his shoulder. "Did you write that, sir?"

"Me? Write this?" Koenig dropped the book, and bent over to pick it up. "Of course not. Why on earth would you ask me that?"

"Frau Schuman's daughter, Rebekah, told me that you read part of a book aloud, last week, at a coffee house. She heard that it was very good. Have you published anything yet?"

Koenig replaced the book on the shelf, fumbling with his glasses.

"Oh, well, I—I don't publish things, Jakob, that's not my interest, you know, not my—oh, there it is!" He pounced upon a newspaper that lay open on his bed, and opened it to the middle section. "I knew I had it somewhere. Here you are, Jakob. Very well-earned, a very nice location." He poured coins into Jakob's open bag. "There you are. Have a nice afternoon."

Reluctantly, Jakob closed up the bag. "Why don't you publish anything, sir?"

"It's—it's really not—ah—how is your mother doing, actually? Your father—such a fine man, what a pity. Is she?"

"She's fine," Jakob said. "Thank you." He backed away, very slowly.

"If you ever need help, Herr Koenig—"

"With writing?"

"No, with—well, with, you know, the, uh, magic...." Jakob let his words drift off, confused by the sudden change in Koenig's expression.

"I do not do magic!" Gasping for breath, Koenig grabbed the rickety bookcase for support. "I—I don't have any idea what you're talking about! I am a scholar. I don't know—I think—you had better leave now, Jakob. I think your mother probably needs you downstairs, don't you?"

Jakob sighed, and turned around. "Yes, Herr

Koenig. Good-bye." He opened the door. Before stepping through, though, he added: "But if you ever need help with anything—"

"Yes, I'll remember. Good-bye!"

As Jakob shut the door behind him, he heard rustling from inside the room. He stood very still, trying not to breathe. A moment later, the low chanting began again. Jakob took a breath, and ran down the stairs. The first wisps of new incense followed him, brushing his nose and hair.

He let himself into the apartment with his heavy, copper key. Inside, it was silent, as always. He set the bag down on the coffee table in the front room, and looked around. Dust gathered on the ornaments his mother had set around the room, and the lace doilies she had crocheted, long ago.

Something looked wrong with the velvet of the long, elegant sofa, but he wasn't sure exactly what it was. He wished he had paid more attention when his mother cleaned, before....

He picked the bag up, and walked through the front room to the door hidden in a corner. He knocked, loudly. After a moment, he opened the door. He clenched his fingers tightly around the handle of the bag. He tried not to cough at the stench of dust and stale air that flooded his lungs as he stepped inside. He tried not to feel afraid.

"Mutti?" he asked. "Mama? It's me, Jakob. Your son."

Slowly, his feet moved forward, shaking clouds

of dust from the heavy carpet.

"I'm opening the window, Mutti, so there will be light in here. That will make you feel better."

He pushed at the thick, dark curtains until bright shafts of sunlight darted in, piercing the darkness. Specks of dust hung in the air, highlighted into gold. The figure on the bed did not move. He walked forward, biting his lip, until he stood directly in front of the large wooden frame of the bed, looking down at the still, narrow shape. He saw her eyes blink, twice. Was it a sign?

"I collected rent today, from Herr Goldberg and Herr Koenig. It's enough to buy us food for another month, and almost enough for a hat for you, if you wanted one. I saw a beautiful hat yesterday. It was my birthday yesterday, I turned eleven. Frau Schuman and her daughters took me to such a beautiful *Konditerei*, it had wonderful cakes and afterwards they took me to see some musicians that were very good, on the corner near the clock in the town square. I saw a hat shop next door that had such nice hats, you would like them so much. It was very proper. Frau Schuman buys her own hats there too, and I counted up the prices and I've been saving for two months now, to get you a really nice present. If I bought you a hat, you would like it, wouldn't you? You could wear it to go out on a walk with me, and you would be beautiful, you would, and we could see the swans on the river, and you would be happy, wouldn't you? You would like it?"

17

Breathing hard, he stopped. The figure on the bed sighed and closed her eyes. With a visible effort, she rolled over, away from him, turning her face to the opposite wall. Jakob swallowed.

"I'll make you soup now, Mutti—onion soup the way you like it. Frau Schuman gave me a good recipe for it last month. I'll make you soup, and you'll feel better."

He closed his eyes for a moment. Then, quickly, clenching his free hand into a fist, he leaned over and kissed his mother on her moist cheek.

She jerked away from him. Jakob straightened.

"I'll be back soon with your soup."

But when he left the room and closed the door behind him, he did not walk straight to the kitchen. Instead, he dropped the bag onto the floor and scrambled up the armchair until he could see out through the high  window. He pushed it open, and breathed in the fresh air in deep gasps.

*Fine. Fine. She's fine. She's....*

He closed his eyes and tilted his face up to receive the fresh breeze. In the distance, he heard the echoing drums of the soldiers, practicing their maneuvers. Under his breath, he hummed part of the march that he had heard them play last month.

*Someday I'll be a soldier, and march, and wear a big long sword.  Someday. She'll be so proud of me when I'm a soldier, when she sees my uniform, she'll come out to watch me and she'll clap like the women I saw yesterday, all admiring the soldiers. She'll be so happy....*

He breathed in the chilly air, and felt it ruffle his long, curly hair and blow against his cheeks until all he could think of were the low, rolling beats of the distant drums and the silver sword that he would someday wear.

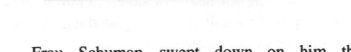

Frau Schuman swept down on him that weekend with both daughters in firm tow, and five baskets full of bread and fruit.

"It's time you ate something fresh in here! Look at all this dust—all the curtains are closed even! Is this a museum? A cemetery? Jakob—no, child, don't run around cleaning things now, it's time for synagogue. No, don't bother your poor mother, I'm sure she won't even notice that we're gone. I'll talk to her later, don't you worry! Anna! Rebekah! Hurry up, children! We'll be late for synagogue, and in times like these the emperor may close it again, for all we know...."

She herded them out, onto the narrow cobblestoned street and into a crowd of hurrying people. Jakob gazed around him, eyes wide at the unaccustomed colors and noises. Some of the cries were in Czech, and only a few recognizable words sounded through. His father had meant to teach him the language this year, but all of their boarders, and his parents friends, spoke German in private, and the few words of Czech that Jakob had to know had been learned through the walks he had once taken with his mother. He wondered now whether he would ever learn the language.

"Come along, child!" Frau Schuman nudged him gently forward. "Will you make us late?"

"Anna! Oh, for heaven's sake." Frau Schuman rushed forward to pull her youngest daughter away from an enticing chocolate shop.

Rebekah, the older daughter, fell into step beside Jakob. Her face was nearly hidden beneath her shawl, but he heard the smile in her voice when she spoke.

"No cakes to eat today, Jakob. What will we do for entertainment?"

Jakob laughed, tentatively, and looked up at her. "Synagogue, Rebekah?"

"Well, I always design dresses in my head during the service, but what do you think about? Uniforms, I suppose? Jakob, you're blushing, I've found you out."

"You won't tell—"

"Silly." She tousled his hair affectionately, and pointed ahead of them. "Look, here we are. See the windows, how they're boarded up on the top floor?"

Jakob narrowed his eyes to look, past the crowd of people entering the small, dark synagogue, up to the windows of the second floor. "So?"

Rebekah withdrew her shawl to flash him a mischievous grin. "That's where the Golem sits, just waiting to eat up little boys. Didn't you know?"

She ran off, following her mother and sister, and Jakob turned slowly to join the line of men. He glanced up at the window again, curiously. What a strange word—Golem....

After the service, he rejoined Frau Schuman and her daughters, where they stood just outside the cemetery, chatting with two older women. A twinge raced through Jakob's body as he glanced into the cemetery, at the worn gravestones. He forced his eyes away from them. No Jews had been buried in that cemetery for at least a hundred years, maybe more. His father's gravestone lay in a completely different part of the city.

"So, this is young Jakob, eh?" The oldest woman pinched his chin between her fingers to raise his face for inspection. "You're taller than the last time I saw you, boy. What ails your mother, to keep her away from our synagogue again today?"

Jakob swallowed, and tried to look away from her piercing eyes. "My mother is quite well, ma'am. Only, she has a headache today."

"Hmm." She turned and exchanged a meaningful glance with Frau Schuman.

"Marta is...." Frau Schuman let her words trail off, nodding significantly at Jakob.

"Hrm." She turned back to Jakob. "Well, you're

a good boy anyway, so behave and take good care of your mother, hopeless though she may be."

"Ma'am!" Jakob jerked away from her hand, outraged.

She cackled. "Good boy. I like your spirit. Now tell me, when I saw you and our Rebekah here coming into synagogue, what were you both so fired up about?"

Jakob felt himself blush scarlet, remembering the beginning of their conversation. "Ah...." He saw Rebekah wrap a fold of her shawl around her face to hide a knowing grin. Suddenly, he remembered a topic that might be safer. "The Golem, ma'am!"

"What?" She pulled back, staring at him. "What nonsense is that?"

"Rebekah said the reason the windows were boarded up was—"

"Rebekah!" Frau Schuman sighed heavily, and took Jakob's shoulder. "We'll leave you now, Frau Bernstein. I apologize for my daughter's behavior. Jakob, we'll take you home now."

She pulled Jakob away, and the two girls fell into step behind her, whispering to each other and giggling. Jakob looked up curiously at the comfortingly firm expression on her broad face.

"What is the Golem, ma'am? Rebekah said it ate little boys, but—"

"Oh, that girl." Frau Schuman rolled her eyes. "Jakob, pay no attention to my daughter's foolishness. The Golem is no concern of yours, nor should it be of hers." She directed her glare behind her, to her daughters.

"Rebekah, a well-brought-up girl knows better than to talk of superstition."

"But, Mutti, what else can I talk about? You forbade me to talk about politics anymore—"

"What does a girl of sixteen know about politics? You should be worrying about preparations for a husband and a household, not—"

"I know that if the Emperor leaves his soldiers here much longer, the Czechs will revolt, just as he feared they would before, and I know every Jewish family in Prague would be in trouble if they won—"

"Won against a Hapsburg? Against Emperor Franz Josef? Against—Oh, Rebekah, you will drive me wild! A few complaints about taxes, about the soldiers—"

"But ma'am, I love the soldiers," Jakob said. "I'm going to be a soldier too when I grow up, and wear the Emperor's colors, and—"

He broke off. All three women were staring at him as if frozen.

"What's wrong? All I said—"

"We all heard what you said, Jakob." Frau Schuman took a deep breath, and released it. "And that's quite enough of that topic! Now, why don't we talk about your house, which is desperately in need of cleaning.

"Anna, you'll work on scrubbing the kitchen while Rebekah and I—"

"But Mutti—"

Anna pushed up to her mother's side to argue, and Jakob fell back beside Rebekah. He glanced up at her shyly, and saw her smiling down at him.

"Tattle tale," she whispered softly.

"I'm sorry! I—"

"Ssh." She touched his shoulder lightly. "I deserved it, if I scared you."

"I wasn't scared. But Rebekah, is the Golem really just superstition?"

"Hmm." She considered for a moment, tapping her finger against her mouth. "I would say—you'll have to decide that for yourself!"

She swooped down to tickle him and then raced ahead to run up the steps of Jakob's townhouse, followed by her mother's cries of protest.

Herr Goldberg greeted them inside, carrying a bundle of newspapers.

"Madam!" He swept off his tall hat and bowed, still standing on the bottom step of the staircase. "And your most beautiful daughters. What a pleasure to find you here today."

"And yourself, Herr Goldberg." Frau Schuman nodded, smiling. "I'm surprised to find you up, out of your familiar chair. Was there an earthquake, to dislodge you?"

He laughed, and returned his hat firmly atop his bushy mane of hair. "Only an internal one, mad-am. I discovered that I could no longer walk from the bed to my chair for the mess of papers on the floor, therefore—"

"I notice your burst of energy did not take you as far as the synagogue." Frau Schuman's voice was firm, but Jakob saw a tell-tale twitch at the corners of her mouth.

"Ah, would that my abominable health did not prevent it." He sighed, tragically, provoking laughter from the two girls. "If only I had a woman's touch in my life, Frau Schuman—real cooking, the way a true artist can provide it—"

"Is that a hint?" She stepped forward and opened the door to Jakob's apartment. "Inside, inside, children! Herr Goldberg," she continued, more loudly, "I plan to spend the next hour cleaning the cobwebs and dust from this apartment, which has been sadly neglected. Afterwards, you are certainly invited to come for a good solid meal, to revive your flagging spirits. And your religion, if it is not far too late for that to be remedied!"

"Madam!" He bowed again, theatrically. "I am honored. Oh—no, Jakob, my boy, don't go inside quite yet! I have a message for you. Our upstairs neighbor of the spectacles and intellectual activities wants you for some errand, I believe. Among the usual assortment of thumps, breaking glass, and foul odors, I heard him call your name, a few minutes ago. When I called up to him, he didn't answer—"

"And of course your ill health prevented you from climbing a few stairs," Frau Schuman inserted, sighing. "Go see to Herr Koenig, Jakob, and be quick about it."

"Yes, ma'am!" Eagerly, Jakob darted up the steps, around Herr Goldberg's bulky figure and past the second floor landing. A visit to Herr Koenig.... He took a deep breath, soaking in the strange fumes that emanated from beneath Koenig's doorway, and knocked, loudly. "Herr Koenig?"

He waited, then knocked again, even louder. "Herr Koenig? It's me, Jakob."

He thought he heard something fall, inside the room. Suddenly worried, he took the large key out of his pocket, and inserted it into the lock. If Koenig was hurt, or unable to move—

The door swung open, shrieking on its hinges. Koenig, who lay sprawled against the wall, clutching a bottle in his hand, looked up blearily.

"Jakob? Why are you here?"

Jakob stepped inside, slowly. Books and papers were scattered across the room, stained with colorful liquid splotches. A thin column of pink smoke hung in one corner, shivering with the breeze from the tiny, open window. Jakob closed the door behind him.

"Can I—can I help you with anything, sir?"

Koenig stared at him for a moment, frowning intensely. "Help—me, Jakob? Why would I need help?"

"Well—your—"

Koenig laughed, shrilly, and raised the bottle to

his lips. "Oh, it's too late for help, Jakob. You should know that by now. Smart boy, clever. Too bad about...." He frowned, and broke off. "I remember now. I wanted you to buy me some wine, but I—I found a bottle, already, behind the bed." He blinked rapidly. "Come sit next to me, boy. I can't see you from here, you're bouncing."

Jakob hurried across the room. He felt his heartbeat quicken with excitement. A chance to really talk to Herr Koenig....He sat down, cross-legged, a few inches away.

"Better, sir?"

"What? Oh...yes, yes. Good boy." Koenig narrowed his eyes, and peered into his bottle. "Good...." His voice trailed off.

"Can I ask you a question, sir?" Jakob leaned towards Koenig. "I heard of something today—a Golem. Is it real?"

Koenig snorted, and took another drink. "Real enough, for all the skeptics. Haven't you seen the window of the synagogue?"

"It's boarded up. Rebekah said—"

"Rebekah? No, no, Jakob. Loew."

"What?"

"Rabbi Loew. A long time ago." Koenig sighed, and set down the bottle. "Back when the Kabbalah was studied with respect, when real scholars—" He broke off. "You don't want to hear about that, though. You're too young. Too sensible. Everyone's too sensible now. No one knows."

"I do want to know! What is—what was the Golem? Who was Rabbi Loew?"

"A rabbi. A scholar. A dreamer." Koenig's words slowed, as his expression became wistful. "He created the Golem out of clay and magic to protect the Jews of Prague in the old days of oppression. Now, in the beginnings of our new oppression—" He laughed, bitterly.

"He—created it? With magic?" Jakob stared into Koenig's lined face, trying to understand. "Did he wave his arms? Or, um, sacrifice—"

"No! No, no, no." In a sudden burst of movement, Koenig threw the bottle across the room. It landed and broke on the opposite wall, with a crash. "No one understands! No one respects—he used words! Words of power, words of belief, words no one should ever use—he carved the greatest word onto the Golem's forehead, and then the weak ones, the cowardly and timid, forced him to smudge it out again, to lock the body away in the attic, to hide it, pretend that it didn't exist...."

"I don't understand. How could a word do that? I thought he used magic—"

"Words are everything. Words make—" Koenig waved his arm extravagantly, and slipped lower against the floor. "They make the world. They have more power than-" He broke off, looking confused. "More than—" He sighed. "How do you think your father died?"

Jakob froze. "I—"

"What did your mother and Goldberg and all those overbearing women tell you? No wait, I forgot—your mother is—"

Jakob found his voice. "It was an accident! A carriage—the driver wasn't looking—Why are you laughing?"

"Words, Jakob. Words." Koenig scrambled forward, through the piles of paper that littered the floor around him. "There are words that—I'd make you a gift, if you wanted it. There's a word that tells truth. But no one really wants to know, they only—"

"You don't know anything about me at all!" Jakob stood up, feeling the cold of anger and fear stiffen his limbs. "Herr Koenig, I think I should go back down to my mother now. I think—"

"Your mother won't even notice you're gone. You think she doesn't know the truth? You think an accident, with a—oh, wait. Here." He retrieved a scrap of paper from beneath a large heap, and handed it to Jakob. "A gift."

Reluctantly, Jakob took it. "But it—it's non-sense. There are so many letters, and shapes, they—"

"Oh, there's a pattern. Don't worry." Koenig sank onto his back in the paper carpet, laughing weakly. "Words of power can't be written just as they are, you know, it's too dangerous. Cross over three each time, though, and once to the left, and you'll see.... Oh, you will truly see...."

Jakob ran to the door, stumbling over paper. "Good-bye, Herr Koenig. I'm leaving!"

"Wait, Jakob!" Koenig lifted himself slightly, blinking. "I forgot to tell you—you can only use this word twice. And every time you use it—you change! Change...change..."

Jakob slammed the door shut to cut off his words. Stifling tears, he raced down the steps, clutching the paper in his fist, followed by wisps of purple smoke.

Jakob kept the paper hidden most of the time in his pockets, where no one could guess at its existence. His skin tingled beside it, a constant reminder. Sometimes, after an hour spent sitting beside his mother's bed, he would retreat into his own tiny bedroom, lock the door, and spread out the wrinkled paper. Cross over three and once to the left.... Almost against his will, his eyes would follow the pattern Koenig had described, and configure one proper letter—a second, a third— Always, he cut himself off by the time he had scanned the first half, breathing hard, angrily crumpling the paper into a ball and then smoothing it out, and refolding it more neatly, to return it to its hiding place. To wait.

Jakob waited for over three weeks, and the paper rested snugly beside his skin on the first

Tuesday of the next month, when he took the money pouch and climbed up the steps of the townhouse to collect rent from his mother's tenants. He stopped on the second floor landing, and knocked on Goldberg's door. He tried to ignore the exotic scents that drifted down from the room upstairs.

"Come in, come in! I never lock my door." Goldberg looked up from his newspaper and frowned as Jakob entered. "You're looking pale, my boy. What ails you?"

"Nothing, sir." The paper burned against Jakob's skin. He swallowed. "I'm perfectly well."

"Really?" Goldberg sighed, and turned his chair towards his desk.

"Well, I hope this month's payment helps to cure you. Try to use some of it for some excitement, for a change—a gift, a treat—"

"Oh!" Jakob stared at the pile of coins. "Yes, sir! Oh, yes!"

"Jakob?"

"The hat for my mother." Jakob felt happiness fill him up, almost lifting him off his feet. "I have enough money to buy it now! Oh, thank you, sir! Thank you!"

For the first time in weeks, he could not feel the pressure of the paper against him as he ran outside, back to the steps. Finally! Even after the money for the grocer, there would be enough. After all the weeks of saving, and planning.... He forced himself to climb the rest of the stairs to Herr Koenig's apartment.

There was no answer when Jakob knocked, and after a moment he noticed the purse on the floor. He picked it up, tentatively, and shook it. Coins jingled against each other. With a grin, he emptied it into the larger pouch, and ran down the steps, listening to the thunder of his own footsteps and laughing. Finally!

He stopped inside his own apartment, to empty out the money pouch, separate out his own savings, and add them to the cache he kept beneath his bed. Perfect! He scooped the money up, and, for the first time in a long time, did not flinch when he passed by his mother's doorway.

"I'll be back soon, Mutti!" he called. "I'm bringing you a gift!"

He made himself slow down when he went outside. The street was filled with vendors, selling fruits and vegetables and jewelry. He squeezed past them, and through the women who surrounded the stalls, bargaining and testing the wares. He had only been to the hat shop once before, but he knew how to find it once he had passed the short brick house where the Schumans lived. The window was open, so he heard Frau Schuman's voice as he passed, and saw her talking to Anna. She lifted her arms in frustration, and said loudly, "Once your sister finally comes home with the fruit...."

He walked forward quickly, so that she wouldn't notice him and stop him. Surely the shop had to be very close now past one street, right on the next ....

The laughter stopped him. It was low, and ugly, and came from an alley nearby, tucked away where he could not see the men who had laughed.

He stopped walking, suddenly frightened, and when he stopped, he heard a gasp and recognized the voice.

"Get away from me!"

One man said, in strangely accented German, "Here's something more interesting than a tavern, eh, Karl? It's a little Jew girl pretending not to like us."

The other man said, "It's all right, sweetheart. You don't need to pretend. We have the day off, and we can spend it all right here with you."

"Leave me alone! I'll—"

Rebekah's voice suddenly broke off into a cry of pain, as a loud crack echoed through the alley. The sound of tearing cloth followed it.

Jakob barreled into the alley. Rebekah's shawl lay on the ground beside her. A tall, fair-haired man in a soldier's uniform held a patch of cloth from her ripped dress casually in one hand, as he smiled down into her face. Another soldier held her hair knotted around his fist. When Rebekah saw Jakob, her eyes widened into pure horror.

"Let her go!" Jakob halted a foot away from them, breathing hard. His mind reeled as he saw their uniforms, absorbed the scene.

*But they were soldiers...they protected.*

"Let her go or I'll kill you!"

The men laughed again. The one who held Rebekah's hair loosened his sword from its sheath.

"I think we've been threatened, Hans. Do you want to avenge our honor?"

"From a little Jewish brat who couldn't even pick up a sword?" The other soldier shrugged, and tilted Rebekah's face up to look into her eyes. "You didn't tell us you had a big strong protector, darling."

Jakob threw himself forward, hitting out with fierce, angry, useless blows. One of the soldiers backhanded him easily, sending him flying onto his back. As he lay, panting, on the cobblestones, the second one approached, and rested the tip of his sword lightly on Jakob's exposed neck.

"Should I kill him, or just scar him a little?" He grinned down at Jakob. "I think he'd look good with a cut or two."

Jakob heard Rebekah moan, softly. Suddenly, his entire world had become a small circle, focused around the blade that touched his throat.

From a distance he heard the voice of the other soldier.

"Don't bother. There are enough pretty girls in this town, prettier than this one even, and not so much trouble."

Slowly, the sword withdrew. Jakob took a deep breath, and then another. The soldier re-sheathed the sword, and looked back at Rebekah,

"Sorry, sweetheart. Maybe another day."

Rebekah's lips moved, but no sound came out.

Jakob had never seen an expression of such pure hatred on anyone's face before.

The soldiers marched out, spurs jangling loudly. Their voices carried back to the alley for a few minutes, and then faded. Jakob closed his eyes.

"Jakob? Are you all right?"

"I'm fine," Jakob whispered. "I'm fine." He stood up, slowly, and looked at Rebekah, at her torn dress and rumpled hair, and the bruises that were beginning to show on her cheek and mouth. "Are you—?"

She closed her eyes for a long moment. "Don't ask."

Jakob picked up his hat from the ground, and looked back toward the street. "I don't understand! They're soldiers! Soldiers are good, and brave, and kind, and there must have been a reason, they can't have just—"

"Stop it!" Rebekah opened her eyes, and shrieked the words, as if she couldn't help it. "Every time you talk about soldiers you're so stupid, you think you want to be a soldier, you think you know. You don't know anything!"

"Rebekah?"

"Don't you know how your father died?"

Jakob stared at her. "No," he whispered. "No, I don't."

"Those soldiers didn't need a reason! They're stupid and ignorant. They're from the provinces and they grew up hearing devil stories about Jews. They

35

grew up hating us! They were bored.... Your father was Jewish—"

"No!" Jakob ran to her, reached up to try to cover her mouth. She brushed his hand away.

"Your father was killed by soldiers! Drunken, ignorant soldiers who were bored and knew that no one would care if they beat a Jew. No one would notice! The men who did it, they were only reprimanded. They were never even imprisoned. They didn't even lose their posts. The police, the Czechs in the government—"

"No!" Jakob grabbed the piece of paper from its hiding place, and opened it up. *Cross three over once to the left...*He yelled the word.

It dropped him to his knees, his head shaking with thunder, and visions unfolding before his eyes.

*His father knew, as soon as he saw the soldiers. Five of them, each from a different direction. The light of drink, and boredom in their eyes. There were no passersby in the dark street, nothing to distract them.*

*He swallowed, and tried to calm his thudding heartbeat. "Can I help you, sirs?"*

*The leader of the group smiled, and knocked his hat off. "Jew."*

*Another soldier slapped him, lightly, on the cheek. "Moneylender."*

*A third hit him hard in the stomach. The last thing he saw was their faces, all gathered above him. Their blows....*

"Jakob?" Rebekah's voice cut in, suddenly frightened, and pleading. "Jakob, I'm sorry I— Where are you going?"

He could barely see through his tears, through the shock. Something—he had to do something, he had to try. Suddenly, Koenig's words filled his head, and he knew what he had to do.

She didn't hear him the first time he said it, so he had to repeat it. "I'm waking up the Golem!"

It would kill the soldiers. It would solve everything. It would make things right again.

"What? Jakob, wait!"

He left her far behind him. His feet pounded the cobblestones. He crashed into people, but didn't hear their curses. He ran forward, clutching the paper in his hand. He ran.

When he reached the synagogue, he didn't see the people he passed, or think to be grateful that there were so few, and that no one followed him. He ran up the stairs, and didn't give up when he found the door locked. He slammed into it, over and over and over again.

*"Jew."*

*"Moneylender."*

*"Little Jewish brat."*

*"Sweetheart."*

*"Now, in the beginnings of a new oppression—"*

He ran back outside and found a large rock. He dragged it up the stairs and hurled it at the door. The fourth time, he heard the crack of splintering wood.

He threw the rock again, and again. Finally, he crawled through the opening he had made, ignoring the pointed shards of wood that dug into his hands and face.

The attic was dark, and he could barely see. He stumbled over boxes, and old, broken furniture. A pile of books tripped him, and he fell forward, landing with a thud on his chin. When he raised his head, he saw it.

It was huge. Jakob's eyes were finally beginning to adjust in the darkness, but he could only glimpse parts of the massive, clay figure. A hand, larger than Jakob's head, dull, dark eyes, the sunken area in the middle of his forehead, where the word had been smudged out.

Jakob gasped, and it became a sob. Now that he had seen the Golem, he could not force his eyes away from it. It sat on the ground, legs stretched out before it, and arms resting by its side. Its head tilted forward, in a parody of sleep. Even though it was sitting down, it was still taller than Jakob, and its presence seemed to fill all the shadows of the attic.

Jakob swallowed, and felt chills race up through his body. It was impossible for the Golem to see him. Wasn't it? He took a deep breath, and forced the images back into his mind—Rebekah, the soldiers, his father....

"Father," Jakob whispered. "I'll make it right."

He scrabbled around him until he found a tool that he could use. It  was a long, metal knife, and when his fingers closed around it, he suddenly knew that it was the one that had been used before. But the word, *the word*, he had to use....

He spoke the word of truth, that Koenig had given him. Roaring filled his head. He lifted the knife, fighting for breath through the pressure that filled his head, his throat, his body. He felt the direction of another man guiding his hand as he lifted it to the Golem's forehead and slowly, laboriously, began to carve the first letter.

The room began to shake. As if from a very far distance, he heard screams from the level below. Footsteps sounded on the steps, but he ignored them. A red haze massed around him, wrapping him and the Golem into a private circle, a separate world.

He heard pounding at the door, and words that he could not understand. There were four letters, in total. He lifted his hand to begin the second.

A deep, red glow began burning within the Golem's sunken eyes. It grew, until it nearly blinded Jakob. He looked away, resolutely, and finished the third letter. He heard wind rushing around him. He thought the roof of the synagogue might be trying to rip itself loose. He began the third letter. The Golem lifted its head, and stared at Jakob. Its hand slowly rose, and then crashed down, breaking a wooden chair.

"Golem?" Jakob heard his voice break as he looked into the Golem's red glare.

He saw hatred. He saw mindless, killing rage.

He tried to jerk his hand away from the forehead. It was too late. He had lost control. He watched his hand carve the rest of the third letter.

"No! No! Stop!" The rising wind sucked away his words, and beat at his face.

Sobbing, he tried to pull away from the monster, but could only watch, helplessly, as his own hand rose to etch the final letter.

"Jakob!"

Hands seized his shoulders from behind. The knife fell from his hands onto the floor, with a sharp, metallic clink. Shuddering convulsively, he jerked around.

His mother stared back at him. Her face was wild. He noticed, with a feeling that surpassed shock, that she was still wearing her nightgown. He stared at her.

"Mutti?"

Rebekah ran forward, past them, her face white with terror. Even while sitting, the monster dwarfed her in size. Its massive head swung towards her, and its arms reached out, each as thick as her body. Jakob cried out, helpless—

She grabbed the blade of the knife that Jakob had dropped, and, in a violent, sudden movement, she pushed the blunt handle into the Golem's forehead. The giant arms halted in mid air as she smudged the carven letters together, into a shapeless indentation. Jakob waited, hardly breathing, as the Golem's arms hung motionless for a long moment,

*He lifted his hand to begin the second letter.*

and its red gaze remained fixed on Rebekah. The wind that had filled the attic disappeared, with a sound like a sigh. Then, with a thud that shook the room, the clay figure collapsed backwards, onto the ground. The red glow in its eyes flickered, and disappeared.

Rebekah dropped the knife, and looked down at her outstretched hand as if it belonged to a stranger.

Jakob looked at both of them, frozen by the sudden silence, and so confused that he felt as if he were floating in a strange limbo. He swallowed, hard, before he spoke. "I—I don't understand."

"I didn't know what to do," Rebekah said. "I knew, I knew if I went to my mother, she would only notice my dress—I didn't—"

Jakob's mother touched his face, with a hand that trembled. "I'm sorry," she whispered. "I am so sorry, Jakob. Can you ever forgive me?"

He stared at her. "But—"

"I left you," she said. "I was so caught up in my grief, I forgot I had a reason to live. Oh, darling—*Liebchen*—I've been such a bad mother, but I do love you so much. When Rebekah came running into my room and told me that you were in danger, that you could be killed, that you had gone to wake the Golem—for the first time, I realized what I had done." She smiled, though tears trickled down her cheeks. "Liebchen, I'm awake now. I'm back."

A slow trembling began deep inside Jakob's stomach, and spread upwards until his whole body was shivering, and his teeth were chattering together, as everything from the past months came together.

"Mutti," he whispered, and his voice broke. "I tried so hard—"

She reached out to him, and drew him into her embrace. "You tried so hard," she whispered. "But you're only a little boy. You can't expect yourself to solve the sins of the world."

He twisted back to look up at her face. "But the Golem was supposed to protect us! Koenig said he was made to protect the Jews, to be our savior...."

His mother's voice was steady. "It's true that he was created for that, but his creator lost control. When Rabbi Loew awakened him, he burst into a killing frenzy—and he attacked not just the enemies of the Jews, but anyone he saw."

Rebekah spoke, quietly, from beside them. "When those men grabbed me, all I wanted was to hurt them, the way they hurt me. But I think—I think if I did, I wouldn't ever feel clean again."

His mother looked at the Golem, who lay motionless only a few feet away, and shivered. "Don't trust a killer to solve our problems, Liebchen."

"But if I can't solve anything," he said, "then why should I even live? How can we keep on living, when so many evil—"

"Shh," his mother whispered. "Shh. That's what I thought, too. But you can't withdraw from the world. There's too much love in it, and too many people to care about." She reached out one arm, and pulled Rebekah into their circle of warmth. "You just have to keep on trying. For their sake."

"But—"Jakob cut off his own question, and took a deep breath.

Rebekah smiled at him, tenderly, and laughed. "Always questions?"

Jakob swallowed. He tried very hard to understand, finally managing to smile back at her. "I think—I think that I can wait until later. Now that....."

He looked over to his mother, and had to remind himself that she was real. She wasn't sleeping, wasn't looking through him as though he were a stranger, wasn't....

She leaned over to kiss him on his forehead.

"Believe me, Liebchen," she whispered. "Even when it all seems hidden, there is so much love in this world. Just remind yourself of that, when you can."

Slowly, Jakob let out the breath he had been holding for what seemed like a very long time. Tentatively, still not quite believing that he could, he leaned into his mother and Rebekah, and let himself absorb their warmth. His mother gently brushed the tears off of Rebekah's cheek, and rested her chin lightly on Jakob's head. As the clay monster slept beside them, the three of them breathed, very slowly, in unison.

# A Dybbuk in
# North Tonawanda

*by Eliot Fintushel*

ELIOT FINTUSHEL is an itinerant showman, among other things. He has won the U.S. National Endowment For The Arts Solo Performer Award, twice. His recent novella, *Izzy and the Father of Terror* was a Nebula Award nominee.

In this story, Eliot takes what might have been simply a well written dybbuk tale and adds a new twist to it. He asks the intriguing question: What is the worst thing that could happen to a dybbuk?

The results may surprise you....It certainly surprised the author.

Maybe you heard the story of Laia, daughter of Hannah, who was betrothed in her heart and in the eyes of God to Chonnon, a poor rabbinical student. Her father made her marry a rich man instead. Poor Chonnon died of grief.

On Laia's wedding day Chonnon's soul entered her body and would not leave. She raved and shrieked in Chonnon's voice. Even the great and famous Reb Azrielkeh of Miropolye could not exorcise the dybbuk Chonnon. All night long the dybbuk defied the great rabbi, weeping Laia's tears and arguing with Laia's tongue. "We are one flesh! We will nevermore part!" By sunrise the poor girl was dead. She had joined Chonnon in the place where dybbuks — dead souls — gather, halfway between earth and heaven.

Of course, there is no such place. Everyone knows that nowadays. Nor is there such a thing as a dybbuk. Probably Laia had a fever. She was delirious. Probably the rabbi had a touch of it himself: something in the water or a fungus on the wheat that makes people lose their hold for a while.

Mass hysteria is what it was, probably, and the next day they all felt very sad and silly.

But pity us poor storytellers. On a diet of facts, the likes of us will starve. Give us a maybe to nibble on, can't you? A draft of suppose? A sip of what-if? Without that, I, impecunious spinner of yarns, Fintushel, son of Izzy, will have to go out and work for a living, chas vesholem: God forbid.

I sit before the word processor (God bless modern living!) in my blue room with the myrtle lamp and the green window shade, scratching my head between paragraphs. Come, a maybe, a suppose, a what-if— honestly, would it kill you?

What if there were such a place as the realm of the dybbuks, a shadowy sphere halfway between earth and heaven? Can't you see it teeming with souls of the dead? (So squint a little!) How they snuggle and squeal, a million in a bunch, flank to flank and snout to tail like puppies in a basket. Only, they haven't any flanks or snouts or tails; they are dybbuks, bodiless souls. That is the point after all: they want bodies. Maybe mine. Maybe yours. Look out!

Suppose there were such creatures as dybbuks. Through the thatch of your succah you could almost see them ghosting past the autumn moon, vaporous and swift. Ordinary people think they are merely clouds, but you and I know better. Back in the house, you close all your windows and lock them tight. You leave a nightlight burning.

Beneath three blankets, a quilt, and a sheet, you can't stop shivering. You cannot turn or tuck enough to feel really safe. In your heart you say a prayer, "Protect us, oh Lord...." But is it your own voice deep down inside you—or a dybbuk's?

Truth to tell—albeit a storyteller's truth—there once dwelled in the realm of the dybbuks, a certain soul called Ishky. Ishky was dead now, of course, but did he like it? Not at all. He would not lie still in the earth, as dead individuals ought to do. Nor would he suffer his spirit to be reunited with his Maker.

No, Ishky—maybe, don't forget my maybe—was only happy when he was wriggling into a live human soul. He was like a hookworm or a tick, was Ishky. A dybbuk. Why? Don't ask! It's an embarrassment, a befuddlement, a shame. Was he tormented like the terrible dybbuk of Minsk who roamed the earth in search of his beloved? No. Was he greedy like the dybbuk of Pinsk—

Spit three times to be free of the curse and the taint of even mentioning him!—who infested the souls of rich men only? No.

Children: that was Ishky's specialty, and the more mischievous the better. Nothing attracted him like laughter. (Careful, now!) Maybe one day, as you squeezed down a narrow crowded street, a baby in a carriage trundled past you in front of its weary mama, and in the warm dark of that carriage you saw such a leer and heard such a yell as no infant ever made. "What are you looking at, fool?" the dybbuk shrieked with the poor baby's tonsils. Then—gone! You looked back. The mother looked back too at you, and in her face you saw despair.

Inside that baby was Ishky.

What did he look like, this evil dybbuk? Don't ask! His face: ashes collapsing in a dead fire. His smirk: threads of flame and plumes of smoke. His laughter: exploding cinders, flying sparks, flaming hair. Even the other dybbuks kept their distance.

Maybe, don't forget. Maybe there was such a one. Let's hope not, but maybe. . .

Suppose there was a human child—a live one, I mean, like yourself. Call him Yossel. One Passover, say, he fell asleep after the second cup of wine, and the prophet Elijah (Ayleeyahoo Hanavee in Hebrew—how melodious!) spied him slumped over the table. Yossel's face was in the chopped nuts. His yarmulke half-covered his eyes. While he snoozed the grownups shmoozed—which is to say: they gossiped—and the children hunted for the afikomon, the hidden matzo. They just let Yossel be, suppose, because they knew he was that way, his own way—sleep when he would, wake when he would, eat, jape, study, jump, et cetera, when he, Yossel, would, und

52

fartik, which is to say: period. Nobody, old or young, would risk Yossel's growl.

Not a soul sees Elijah float in through the open door with a sack slung over his shoulder, not a soul besides you and me, even though it's been left open for just this purpose. They think it's an empty ritual. Nobody sees him stroke his forked beard, white as hoarfrost, and cluck his tongue over Yossel. Nobody sees Elijah scoop our boychik into the sack—plunk!—like onions and potatoes.

Besides myself, you are the only witness.

Watch Elijah walk straight out the open door looking neither left nor right. How does he step so lightly with all those onions and potatoes? His feet barely touch the floor: they seem to float above. Just as he reaches the threshold, Elijah, sack, and onions and potatoes, bubble like ginger-ale. Then they become translucent, like the gel that gefilteh fish comes packed in. You can see the street lamps shine through them. The shimmering blob of them slithers across the porch and fades into the night— gone!

Gone to where? Don't ask!

All right, you've twisted my arm!

Where Elijah ended, I can't say, but he passed through a certain place, suppose, halfway between earth and heaven. There, as the gefilteh fish gel of Elijah the Prophet shimmied twixt the waters below and the waters above, as the first book of Moses describes them, right there, where dybbuks tickle and itch, what if our Yossel, dreaming in the sack, tickling and itching his own tickle and itch, poked a little hole?

We know how it goes with little holes, don't we? They grow bigger. As Elijah ascended from sphere to sphere, stars in his hair now, satellites in his beard—here a Sputnik, there a Hubbell—ozone in and out of his ears, Yossel, still sleeping, worried that hole bigger and bigger. At last, as you expected, he onioned and potatoed himself out of the sack and—plunk!—among the teeming dark souls of the dybbuks.

He was half-shod now: one shoe stayed in Elijah's sack, a brown loafer. It's there to this day, and if you don't believe me just pretend to fall asleep next seder so you can catch a glimpse of old Elijah. Make sure to place yourself where the hoary old prophet will have to pass between you and a lamp. In that sack of his you'll see the shadow of Yossel's shoe, or I'm no storyteller.

Yossel's yarmulke stayed on his head. His Paisley necktie stayed around his neck, his stiff white shirt stayed on his shoulders, and his itchy wool pants stayed on his legs. Thank goodness he had shed his good sports jacket, and it was hanging on the back of his chair at the seder table way down on earth, so at least that item was spared the wear and tear of the upper stratosphere.

You'll excuse me, but I forgot: have we supposed anything further about Yossel yet, about what sort of a mensch he might be? Aside from being willful and mean, of course. No? Let's do that now, while his Paisley tie remains around his neck—it won't for long. How about a little story to illustrate his character?

What if Yossel was the scourge of cats, the terror of pigeons, the tormentor of dogs? What if he liked to swing one by the ears, clip the wings of another, and tie cans to the tail of a third? Did he pick his father's pocket, steal his best friend's bicycle, short-sheet his own mother, and paint his schoolteacher's seat with contact cement?

Actually, no.

But give me a break. I'm a storyteller.

Suffice it to say, old Yossel was a world-class meshuggener, which is to say: a pain. Suppose.

Here, then, see Yossel, prince of meshuggeners, tumbling among dybbuks in a hazy between-world. Up and down are scrambled. Souls are as jumbled as bunjee jumpers in zero-G. All around poor Yossel they heave and rumble like beans in the belly—and trumpet and stink the same way. Yossel rolls to the right: something leaps, sprouts oily black wings, and flies away. He rolls to the left: a thousand cockroaches grow tongues and chant the names of the dead. Is he mortified? Is he petrified? Does he tremble and cower?

Not on your life! The meshuggener laughs. His laughter, a child's laughter, rings through the dybbuk realm, and who should prick up his blackened ear, brittle as matzo, touchy as a sunburn? Of course, it would have been our Ishky. Would have been. This is all what-if, remember. What-if, suppose, and maybe.

Don't forget.

Up rears Ishky. Gas fumes to a match is Yossel's laughter to Ishky. The dybbuk Ishky, with an evil smirk, zeroes in on Yossel. Is it a tornado? No, it's Ishky preparing to drill into Yossel's soul!

Only, Yossel does him one better. The meshuggener hops, skips, and jumps from butt to back to horned head of twenty teeming dybbuks, straight into Ishky's bloody maw. He slingshots around one monstrous eyetooth, ducks under an epiglottis as huge and horrible as Mammon's gut, and slides down the dybbuk Ishky's throat. "Wheee!"

The dybbuk gulps. The dybbuk shudders. The dybbuk cocks his horseradish head and furrows his sausage brow. "Huh?"

Imagine: through the murk and mist of the dybbuk realm, the creatures gather. Some slime- like slugs, some arrow-like bats, some trundle-like garbage trucks on flat tires.

"Ishky, vos vaynstu? What's your problem?"

"Ishky, how come the face?"

"Oy, Ishky! You look like someone just danced on your grave."

Ishky opens his mouth to speak, but out comes Yossel's voice: "I'm not Ishky. I'm Yossel. Yossel! And now this body belongs to me." Such a tumult

*Yossel rolls to the right.... He rolls to the left*

you never heard. The dybbuks' mouths open like volcanoes. They slap their hands, their paws, their wings, their scabrous talons to their cadaverous cheeks and wail. "Vay is mir! Woe unto us! Who has ever heard of such a horror? Our Ishky is possessed by a human!"

"That's right," Yossel pipes up, and it practically reams poor Ishky's throat. "And you can bet I'm not leaving anytime soon. It's cozy in here. And that seder was so boring!"

Wasn't Yossel having a wonderful time? (Well, no. It's a maybe, remember, a bobbe-myseh I'm concocting, which is to say: a yarn. But cut us some slack, ey?) He was like a baby with a brand new rattle: shake it this way, shake it that, see what the doodad can do.

The poor dybbuk cannonballed through heaven thumbing his nose at the Ancient of Days: it was Yossel's doing. Ishky found himself winging over heaven and under hell, dropping everywhere little white gifts of the sort that pigeons like to distribute: all, all Yossel's doing! Back among the dybbuk hordes, Yossel made Ishky curse and yowl. He broke every friendship, such as it was, that Ishky had ever made, and he acquired dozens of new enemies.

Then, to top it all off, Yossel, like a wacky astronaut in the cockpit of Ishky's innards, zoomed down into his very own living room. There were the children still poking under cushions and peeking into cupboards, and there the elders kibitzing. Yossel maneuvered Ishky like a Stealth bomber. He read the dybbuk's supernatural mind as if it were an instrument panel. In two seconds he had the afikomen in his crosshairs, and—hooha—he scooped it up and spirited it away like a doggie bone, lightly, between the dybbuk's teeth.

What did Yossel's family see? The curtains fluttered. Lights flickered, and candles smoked. Bubbe Sophie's sepia portrait in the gilt frame on the TV set—she with the prune face and the faint mustache—shot into the air, revealing behind it the sought-after matzo. It whirled. It levitated. Bubbe crashed, and glass shattered. The afikomen floated out the door, still open for Elijah—they didn't know he'd come and gone.

They heard the unmistakable sound of Yossel laughing, laughing the way a person might laugh who had a matzo between his teeth and who didn't want to drop it or get it wet. Then they looked at Yossel's place at the seder table, at their empty chair where his jacket was draped.

To the stunned family Uncle Morris announced in a voice numinous and deep: "A dybbuk!"

"Oy-oy-oy," cried Yossel's mother, "my little son is possessed by a dybbuk."

"Not quite," said Morris, who had been a rabbinical student in Lithuania before becoming a Laundromat attendant in Detroit. "The laughing, the throwing, the monkeyshines—the dybbuk is possessed by our Yossel."

"It's not fair," whined Yossel's kid sister Mollie. She had been reaching to look behind Bubbe Sophie just when the bad wind blew in. "He gets to have all the fun and the afikomen too."

"Sha, Mollie," said the mother (let's suppose.) "Morris, what can we do?"

Said Morris: "There is only one thing poor mortals like ourselves can do when we are confronted with such a phenomenon. There is only one way to save our Yossel, one person whom we can trust to mediate between the two worlds, ours and the dybbuk realm. I speak of the descendent of the great line of rabbis issuing from Reb Azrielkeh of Miropolye, who stood face to face with a dybbuk in the body of Laia, daughter of Hannah, anciently, Brinnits. I speak of the great Rabbi Max, son of Seymour."

"Max, son of Seymour, you say? Must we fly to Brinnits, then? To Miropolye? Moscow? Jerusalem?"

"North Tonawanda."

"North Tonawanda? How could such a wise and holy man as Reb Max abide in a place like North Tonawanda? They make juke boxes in North Tonawanda. How North Tonawanda?"

"Sporting goods."

"Ah."

They only paused to sweep up the glass and to right Bubbe Sophie's picture on the mantelpiece, and off they sped, straight to North Tonawanda, a

**61**

hundred miles on the New York State Thruway, one stop before Niagara Falls. "It's life or death," said Morris, "or I'd never let you drive on a holiday."

From the back seat, between Rochester and Lockport, he rang up Reb Max on his cellular. Morris rang and rang until, Passover or no, the good rabbi finally picked up.

"Voos? A dybbuk? And who's in who? Oy-oy-oy! Ashes and blood! Of course I will help you. Only, mind, I've had my fourth cup of wine. You may have to prop me up."

I, storyteller, Fintushel, son of Izzy, son of Mendel, tap on the letter keys and drum on the space bar while night falls and my green window shade darkens. Here I sit with my dictionaries and my dog-eared papers and my coffee cups, one, two, three, because I'm in too much of a frenzy to wash one. But for Yossel's family it was ten at night, huddled in a Ford station wagon with fake wood paneling and a perforated muffler.

It was just before midnight, say, when the family found the great rabbi's residence. Papa, Mama, Mollie, Morris, Aunt Sadie, who was Morris's wife, a hefty matron with three gold teeth and a heart condition, and also the cousins, two boys and a girl—or the other way round if you like—peered into the night, fogging the windows of the ancient rusting station wagon that dieseled for ten minutes after Papa turned it off. They saw the sign on the dry goods store a few blocks from the Wurlitzer organ and juke box factory: "Eppes Maximus." Reb Max lived upstairs over the Maximus in a one-room apartment with a goldfish.

Papa, Mama, Mollie, Morris, Aunt Sadie, who was still Morris's wife, and the cousins, however many and whatever proportion of genders, marched up the narrow staircase and filed in through the rabbi's door: smack, smack, smack on the mezuzah, the little tin aslant the doorpost, which to kiss was equivalent to a little prayer. Morris wasted no time in explaining exactly what had transpired, while Mama punctuated with here an oy! and there an ...ai! Aunt Sadie sobbed so constantly that you would have expected her heart to plotz on the spot, which means—well, untranslatable, but it wouldn't be tidy. Papa groaned. Mollie snickered. The cousins watched the goldfish.

It's true, or let's say so anyway, that Reb Max, son of Seymour, seemed a little tipsy. His whiskers were so wild and tangled that a princess might find Moses in a basket between his chin and jowls. Where you could glimpse the rabbi's face it was bright red. His enormous gray eyes were half-closed. His lips, inside that forest, that lowland marsh of a face, were as plump and round as if he were perpetually pronouncing the letter "o." He wore a white shirt, a tunic really, very old-fashioned, with ruffled sleeves. Black suspenders held up his trousers. The fringe of his little prayer shawl showed above the empty belt loops where the shirt wasn't quite tucked in.

A real sight.

"Nu?" The great rabbi was reclining, as is commanded on Passover. The site of his reclination was a Lazyboy, with his feet up, his shoes off, and three toes wiggling through the holes in his socks. Maybe four. "So are we exorcizing or are we exorcizing? Bring me my kittel: my good white robe. Hang up a bed sheet across the bay window. And could somebody wash the dishes, please? Who can concentrate with all this chozzerai?" Which is to say: a mess.

Imagine it done, the dishes clean and stacked, a bright white bed sheet tacked up like a tent flap across the window nook and strangely illumined by a street lamp, "aglow" you might almost say. And there is Reb Max, stunning—and vertical!—in his ceremonial robe, which shines so silky white it would give a person a headache to even look at it. Still, he wobbles, and Morris has to give him a shoulder to lean on.

"This is the great rabbi?" Mollie joins the cousins at the goldfish bowl. "Hoo-boy! This doofus couldn't exorcise goo from a zit. From now on, thank God, I'm an only child."

"Ghi diddy di!" Tipsy or no, Reb Max raises his arms, as Moses did at the battle of Rephidim, and he chants a holy chant. So impressive is the sound of that chant, suppose, so full of passion, that Papa, Mama, Uncle, and Aunt, pop-eyed and slack-jawed, are riveted. The cousins stare. The goldfish presses its nose to the glass. Even Mollie inclines an ear.

"Oh ye dybbuks of the nether world, of the invisible realm between earth and heaven, ye wandering dead souls, hear me. I, Rabbi Max, son of Seymour, son of Irving, son of Shmuel, son of Melvin, Max of North Tonawanda, Max of Eppes Maximus, 'where a penny's worth a nickel,' I summon you! Come forth!"

As nothing happens, the rabbi whispers in Mollie's ear to fetch from the kitchenette a jar of pickled herring and some Passover candies, colored half-moons of gelid sugary stuff. Lay them out on plates and slip them under the sheet onto the window ledge, he says, and quick.

Something funny. By all appearances Reb Max has drunk not four cups of wine but four gallons, drunk it, gargled it, and bathed in it, but on the rabbi's breath does Mollie sniff a hint of wine? She does not. "Old faker, why do you pretend to be tipsy?"

"Sha!" he whispers. "If the evil spirits believe I am sober, me with my pedigree from Brinnits, do you think they'll show themselves? In a pig's eye!" He hiccups loudly, then winks. Mollie grins. She collects the shmaltz and the sweets and slips them onto the window ledge. Their shadows fall across the bed sheet.

The rabbi calls out, "I summon you, dybbuks! Come already. Have a little what-to-eat." At these last words the bed sheet ripples as if in a cyclone. Suddenly the room fills with unearthly whispers in exotic tongues and a ghastly buzzing sound. The cousins cover their ears in fright. At first it seems that the street lamp has gone out, because the entire bed sheet darkens, but by degrees the shadow dwindles and separates into a hundred smudges, then spots, then speckles jumping and teeming around the shadows of the shmaltz herring and the half-moon sweets.

"It's okay," a tiny voice says, "he's tipsy."

As the speckles swarm, the shadows of the food diminish. "The food itself they can't touch," says the Rabbi, *sotto voce*, "since they are spirits. But the shadows of the food, that they gobble— you'll excuse the expression—like pigs."

In a moment, the bottom of the sheet curls up, and out come the plates with the food still on them. Mollie's little forehead wrinkles. "But, Rabbi, they haven't touched it."

"No? Look." In truth (but remember, please, what these words mean on a storyteller's tongue) the shmaltz and the sweets are untouched, but their shadows are completely gone. Mollie lifts the plates and turns them in the light, but however she holds them, they cast no shadow.

"Dybbuks, hear me!" In his fervor the rabbi clutches Morris's shoulder. The big man winces. In the morning there will be marks from the rabbi's fingernails. "Dybbuks, have you among you one who is possessed by a living child?"

From behind the sheet, an infernal chorus intones, "Funny you should mention it. Our Ishky has got himself quite a bundle. He was a devil before, and now he's worse. Even we dybbuks cower before him. Can you help us—and do you have any more of that herring?"

The rabbi nods to Mollie, and she runs into the kitchenette. She has just returned with fresh plates when, from behind the sheet, a familiar voice booms: "You doofuses, you think you can budge me? Me, Yossel, son of Milton? I know what you're up to, and I'm not going anywhere. It's comfy in here. I'm king of the place. And what's more, I've got the afikomen. Nyaah, nyaah!"

The cousins burst into tears. Aunt Sadie embraces them. Yossel's mother too tries to embrace her boychik, through the sheet of course, like a hot pot through an oven mitt, but Reb Max waves her off. "This sheet of mine divides the worlds above and the worlds below the firmament. No soul may violate this boundary and live."

Just then the dybbuk Ishky gets hold of his

own tonsils long enough to screech, like a chicken in a sack: "Save me, Rabbi. I can't take it anymore. Deliver me from this vicious creature, and I promise never to possess another living soul. I'm through with the whole business, believe me."

Yossel's mother notices her husband sampling a morsal of de-shadowed herring and casts a menacing look in his direction. Reader, shame to tell, Milty has been smiling, thinking about life without the meshuggener. No more cans of itching powder inside his slippers. No more thumbtacks on his easy chair. Time to relax and read the paper, maybe . . . but at his wife's glance he blanches. He looks down.

"Nu? Nu?" Yossel's mother gives the great rabbi's kittel a tug. "So will you get my Yossel back already?"

What if the rabbi nods gravely? What if he takes a deep breath, gathering his strength? Suppose the air darkens, thickens, curdles. Sparks fly from the rabbi's forehead. Morris is thrown back as by a fallen power line.

And what if the rabbi should thunder, "Yossel, son of Milton?" Suppose he clasps both hands before him in a holy secret sign known only to himself and to Rabbi Loew of Prague, long dead, who with this same sign brought to life a Golem, a man made of clay—let's say. "Yossel, son of Milton, by the light and by the dark and by Him Who made them both, by the power of lightning,

by the power of floods, by the power of the
Wurlitzer plant a mere block away, which produces
organs and juke boxes that can't be beat . . . "

"Reb Max?" ventures Milton.

"Sorry, Milton, it's the lateness of the hour
and that fourth cup of wine—where was I?"

"Lightning and floods."

"Ah. By lightning, by floods, by hurricane
and hisicane and Novocain and Abel-and-Cain, by
the bumps in the matzo and the bones in the chick-
en, I, Max, son of Seymour, son of Irving, son of
Shmuel, son of Melvin, the chosen representative
of the congregation here gathered, including espe-
cially Yossel's own dear mama, I, Max, a genuine
bonafide rabbi, command you, Yossel, son of Milton, to fly out from the poor dybbuk  Ishky's gut
and come before us now, on our side of the bed
sheet, never to leave us more."

The bed sheet flutters.  The bed sheet roils.
The bed sheet flaps and snaps like a whip.  The
shadows of all the terrified dybbuks swarm to one
corner where they huddle and quake.  For a
moment—dreadful silence.

Then, from behind the bed sheet: "Fooey!"

Yossel/Ishky's shadow grows until it fills the
entire sheet, imagine.  Maybe he is moving back
toward the window, toward the light—why?  Then,
swiftly, the shadow shrinks again.  He is rushing
the barrier.  It swells like a topsail in a typhoon and
gives the rabbi such a smack that he lands flat on

his bottom, with Morris behind him in a similar condition.

The sheet hangs straight again, except for the ripples of Yossel's laughter. "You pipsqueaks can't do a thing to me. I'm king of the place, I tell you."

As the live humans, aghast, huddle round him, Reb Max sits on the floor and shakes his head. "It seems we are helpless. I don't understand how such a thing could have happened. In the six thousand biblical years since Adam and Eve, was such a thing ever heard of? That a living soul should possess a dybbuk instead of the other way around? I confess I don't know what to do."

"So you're a boozehound after all." Mollie leans over Reb Max and shakes her fist. "I suppose you'll let my brother just stay there and make everybody more miserable than ever. I suppose you're going to sit on your bottom while the meshuggener laughs. I suppose we have to just stand here and put up with it."

The rabbi raises one eyebrow and looks up at her. "That's a lot of supposing for one little girl."

"Maybe he'll turn heaven itself upside-down—you don't know Yossel like I do. Maybe he'll whip the dybbuks into an army and take over the whole wide world. Maybe he'll make himself out to be God Almighty. What do you care, am I right?"

"Such a lot of maybes! Where do you get

them?" The rabbi cocks his head.

"And what if he pinches me?"

"And now a what-if!" All at once Reb Max's eyes widen. "Suppose! Maybe! What if!" He smacks his forehead with the heel of his hand. "It sounds like a story!"

"A story?" says Mollie.

"A story?" says Morris.

"A story?" say Mama, Papa, and Aunt Sadie.

(The cousins are back to the goldfish.)

"A story?" say the dybbuks all in a chorus, infernally discordant, as befits them, all but Ishky, whom Yossel makes say,

"Fooey!"

"Of course!" Rabbi Max rises to his feet like a mountain rising from the primeval earth. "A story. A myseh. A bobbe-myseh. How could I have missed it? Suppose! Maybe! What if! I should have smelled a rat—I mean a storyteller— the instant Morris gave me his dizzy account. A child inside a dybbuk, indeed!"

Before Morris can restrain him, Rabbi Max, son of Seymour, of the line of the estimable Azrielkeh of Miropolye, has mounted the seder table. With one foot on the seder plate and one foot next to a bottle of Manischewitz, he raises his hands so high and bellows so loudly that dybbuks and humans alike shut their eyes and cover their ears.

In fact—such as facts are, remember, for an

old storyteller—Reb Max raises his hands so high that they burst through the ceiling of his little apartment over Eppes Maximus, through plaster and laths and floorboards and tile and across seven universes and twenty-six impossibles straight up into my own blue room, mine, Fintushel-son-of-Izzy's room. Reb Max's hands crash out next to the end table with the myrtle lamp, which tumbles over, leaving me in darkness.

Quickly, I grope for a candle and a match. No maybes in that, reader. I have to see what's going on, what monkeyshines is this. Everywhere, there's sawdust and splinters and the sound of an old man roaring: "You, storyteller, by the power and authority of my ancestor rabbis, the ancient great ones, as well as by the dictum of Hillel himself, who declared that no one should do to somebody what he wouldn't want done to himself, I command you...."

"You command me?" I say. Old Max chins up through my shattered floorboards. Now he's standing on Morris's shoulders. "I created you, you ingrate, you gornisht: you nothing."

I pull a manuscript from my desktop—this page, in fact—and brandish it in Reb Max's face as if it were an eviction notice.

The rabbi is unimpressed. "According to our sacred law, even God Most High has certain obligations to His creatures. How much more so a mere pencil wagger like yourself! I demand that you undo the shameful and ridiculous situation that you have created. I demand that you free the dybbuk Ishky from possession by the human child Yossel. I demand that you cause this Yossel to be returned unto the bosom of his family. It's Passover—let our Yossel go!"

"That's all?" I say.

"Well, a little more shmaltz wouldn't hurt. The dybbuks ate up all the shadows, and without the shadows, frankly, I find it a bit flat."

"I know what you mean."

"So you'll do it?"

"The herring? Done. A whole case of twelve-ounce jars, big ones, complete with shadows. Now go."

"And Ishky? And Yossel?"

"You'll forgive me, Rabbi, but you're making me a little bit nervous. You belong on the page, not on the floor. Please go."

"Not until you rewrite."

"I wrote you—I banish you! You creature of ink, you what-if, you maybe, I exorcise you back into the ink cartridge, into the LCD screen."

"Nu? So now I am the dybbuk? No, Fintushel, son of Izzy, it is I who exorcise you." He tears the manuscript page from my hand. "Begone, teller of tales. I'll take over from here." He shoulders past me, stirring up sawdust with the hem of his kittel, and he plunks himself down at my desk. Spurning my PC, he picks up a pencil and begins to write.

What can I do? Haul him bodily into the paper shredder? Rub him all over with an eraser? I am not a violent man—well, only in my imagination. I peer over Reb Max's shoulder. Here is what he writes:

"Truth to tell, as the wise and holy rabbi, Max, son of Seymour, strove against Fintushel, son of Izzy, a terrible lamentation was heard. Yossel, moved at last by his mama's tears, wailed and wept. He leapt out of the dybbuk's mouth and ducked under the bed sheet that separated the two worlds.

"Yosseleh, beloved son!" cried his mama.

"Mama, dear!" cried Yossel.

They embraced.

"On the other side of Reb Max's bed sheet the dybbuks sighed. 'Rabbi,' they said, all in a chorus, 'because of your goodness and power, our Ishky has been freed of his burden, and we dybbuks are so happy that not a single one of us will ever enter a human soul again. As a sign of this covenant we make with you this day, we will deliver unto you a dozen jars of the finest shmaltz herring complete with shadows every Sunday for the rest of your life—and this is in addition to anything that meshugge storyteller is giving you."

Reb Max stares at the green window shade for a minute and then continues to write: "And we will arrange through our occult powers that Eppes Maximus does a brisk trade."

"The dybbuks vanished. The bed sheet fell into a perfectly folded pile, as clean as the day the rabbi had bought it. Instantly, the washed dishes were put away, the floor was swept and mopped, the walls had a fresh coat of paint, and a dozen very large orders for expensive merchandise slipped themselves under the door...."

"Laying it on a bit thick, aren't we?" I say.

Reb Max growls and writes on: "And they all lived happily ever after."

"What about Mollie?" I say.

He writes: "Including Mollie."

"I was getting fond of her," I say. "Couldn't you write a word more?"

He mutters something in Yiddish, and he writes: "Mollie in particular." Then he says, "Here, I'll even give her the afikomen." And he writes a little more.

"I suppose I'll have to be satisfied with that."

"Satisfied, nothing. You're lucky you got off so easy. What if I give you the punch in the nose you deserve? I have half a mind to excommunicate you, as my ancestor Reb Azrielkeh did to the terrible dybbuk of Brinnits."

"No, no, Reb Rumpelstiltskins, Mr. Son of Seymour, Son of Shmuel, Son of Melvin, son of my own fevered imagination. I beg you to forgive me my lies as I forgive you yours. Now, back through the floor with you! Go back into the place that never was, complete with folded bed sheet and freshly painted walls."

"Okay," says Reb Max, "but you're getting off easy."

He writes two more words, exactly two, then jumps down through the hole in the floor straight into Morris's arms. I hear laughter and backslaps and sloppy kisses as the floor heals, the sawdust un-scatters, and the end table rights itself with the myrtle lamp on top glowing as before.

Around the edges of my green window shade sunlight is stealing in. I look down at Reb Max's page, at the two words he wrote before jumping through the floor. I read:

*The End*

*And who am I to say otherwise?*

# Lip Service

*by Yaacov Peterseil*

Science fiction often encompasses the realm of outer space. As a trekke, I longed to go "where no man has gone before." But over the years I've found inner space just as exciting. Sometimes it's just as thrilling to imagine what it would be like to go where man has gone before.

In this story, written before the bris of my first grandson, I try to find the solution to a particular problem which is the subject of the traditional Shalom Zachor held the first Friday night after a Jewish baby boy is born.

**H**ave you ever wondered why there is a slight indentation just above the center of your upper lip?

The Jewish Sages consider every part of the human body sacred, the upper lip being no exception. So, after scrutinizing the upper lip indentation, the conclusion reached by the Sages is that someone—or something leaves its fingerprint on the upper lip of every fetus, as though sealing something within.

But what could this indentation be hiding?

This question goes well with another question the Jewish Sages ask: What does the fetus do during its nine months in the womb? Surely, it cannot be just wasting time...just growing? It must be doing something more, something more...Jewish.

So, what else would a Jewish child be doing in the womb but learning Torah. Surely, argue the Sages, God must appoint one of His heavenly servants to teach the fetus the Torah. After all, that is the purpose of the Jewish people: to know and live God's Torah.

But then how does one explain the fact that

*Jewish newborns seem blissfully unaware of the Torah, much as do their non-Jewish counterparts. (There seems to be no recorded answer to the larger question of: What does a non-Jewish child learn in his mother's womb? After all, non-Jewish children have an indented top lip too.)*

*The answer is quite simple: The same angel that teaches the fetus the Torah is directed to wipe out all the Torah knowledge the fetus has acquired, just before the little one enters this world.*

*How is this done?*

*By putting an angelic finger on the top of the almost newborn's lip. Of course, the real question one must ask here is obvious: Why would God have an angel teach the fetus the Torah, if this knowledge will be erased from the little one's memory anyway?*

*The answer to this question has traveled by word of mouth for ages. It is repeated at every Shalom Zachor, the special ceremony that occurs on the first Friday night after the Jewish newborn boy enters this world. It is part of Jewish tradition, Jewish folklore, and the Jewish Weltanschauung. So you might as well hear it too.*

*The fetus has to forget all the Torah it is taught in order to give the Evil Inclination, called the Yetzer HaRah, a fair chance to influence the baby once the infant enters our world. In that sense, God is the original Equal Opportunity Employer, allowing both the Good Inclination, called the Yetzer HaTov, and the Evil Inclination, equal time.*

*However, all too often, Evil seems to have a slight edge over Good (You never hear of a child giving-in to his Good Inclination, do you?). So, God, in His infinite wisdom, has decreed that as the child grows in this world, and begins learning Torah, he will experience that deja vu feeling that comes from knowing you once knew something, but have somehow forgotten it. Having once learned Torah, the lingering affect of this knowledge, the "taste of Torah" will always be in the back of the child's mind. This will energize the child and stimulate him to learn more Torah.*

*Of course, when the time comes to forget the Torah, it is assumed that the fetus will willingly extend his upper lip for the Angel of God. Then, with one sweep of his finger, the angel will draw out the Torah he has given to the fetus. That's the plan. And, normally, that's how it goes.*

*But the best made plans of mice, men, and angels sometimes. . . .*

"Stop! I don't want to forget all the Torah I've learned," complained the fetus. The little guy had been cooking for almost nine months, and the Angel Who Sends Forth was preparing to touch him on his upper lip.

"No one likes to forget their Torah," admitted the Angel, clenching his fist so as not to frighten the fetus. "But God, in His Infinite Wisdom, has ordained what's good for you. You've been a very attentive pupil, and I have no doubt that as soon as you are born and start talking, you'll pick up all this Torah knowledge again."

"But I'm happy here, and as Rabbi Akiva says—"

"Now, now! Don't start giving me Talmudic reasoning! I only threw Talmudic Law into your studies because you seemed so eager to learn, and we had some time on our hands since you went to full term. That's all behind us now. I expect you to forget about everything, including Talmudic Law."

"But I can't!" burped the fetus. He was having one of those burping fits that so annoyed his mother.

"Well, don't worry," the Angel assured him, "I'll make sure you forget it all."

"NO-URP!" burped the fetus, as determined as ever.

The Angel Who Sends Forth smiled. This was not his first Forth Sending. And this was not his first stubborn fetus.

"I remember another little tike like you," reminisced the Angel. "It must have been well, over 2,000 years ago. He didn't want to forget his Torah, either. He was a sly one, he was.  He promised he wouldn't tell anyone that he knew the entire Torah. All he wanted, like you, was for me NOT to touch his lip. He pleaded and begged and even used some of the Talmudic logic you were going to spout. Tell you the truth, he was very convincing — very, very convincing.

"In those days,"  continued the Angel, self consciously, "I was a beginner at this Sending Forth business. I had just been appointed after the old Angel Who Counts Souls overstepped HIS bounds, and put two souls into one person."

The fetus stopped burping. Truth be told, he was a little scared. It suddenly dawned on him: Could the new Angel Who Counts Souls have made the same mistake and put two souls into him?

"How do you know if you have an extra soul?" interrupted the fetus.

"Burping," answered the Angel without batting a wing. (Even an angel has to have a sense a humor to work with kids!)

The fetus looked wide-eyed at the Angel. His mother felt her stomach tighten, painfully. But the burping went away.

"Just joking," said the Angel, calming the fetus. "They were identical twins and the Angel Who Counts Souls touched the same body twice.

But don't get nervous, mistakes like that only happen once in an Angel's lifetime. It could never, ever happen again."

"Why?" asked the fetus.

"Toe curls," the Angel explained. "The Angel Who Counts Souls is required to keep a file on the way each little one's right big toe curls in the womb. Interestingly, no two fetus' have the same toe curl. That holds true for twins as well. So it's impossible to make such a mistake again.

"But to get back to my story. The problem was that one twin had both souls."

"Why didn't the Angel take out one of the souls?" wondered the fetus, still a little anxious.

"You've got a real Talmudic head, all right," the Angel told him, proudly. "But each Angel has his or her job. One Angel wouldn't dream of doing some other Angel's job. Once the Angel Who Counts Souls doubled-up on a body, he couldn't take out either soul."

"So, why not get the Angel Who Gets The Souls Out or whatever you call him, to take out one soul?" suggested the fetus.

"You're a little sharpie, you are," said the Angel, patting the fetus' face.

The fetus lunged back in surprise, putting pressure on his mother's stomach, which caused her the worst case of indigestion she had experienced since the beginning of her pregnancy.

"Don't worry, I'm not touching your lip, yet,"

*" You've got a real Talmudic head, all right..."*

soothed the Angel. "I never touch a lip without fair warning. But to get back to your question: There is no Angel Who Gets The Souls Out. At least, that's not what he's called. When you call that Angel, well, he gets the soul out...permanently."

The fetus understood, gulped and froze in place. His mother called his father and announced that she was having a very strong contraction.

"So, talk about dybbuks," smiled the Angel. "The double-souled baby entered the world and soon showed what a troublemaker he could be. He ate for two. He cried for two. He even, well, let's just say, he had to be changed for two."

"Was the other one born...?" The fetus let the question fade.

"God forbid!" said the Angel. "He was given a Temporary Soul. That's a soul that will be used in the future, but is free right now. Temporary Souls utilize very little energy until fully activated which meant that the semi-souled kid was quite listless. The parents couldn't believe how one child was so active and the other so passive. By the time we received the Special One Time Right To Return A Soul To Its Rightful Owner (don't ask what that took), the parents were sure they had a full-fledged Frankenstein on their hands. By the way, that Golem had a similar problem."

"But I thought you said this was a one-time problem," the fetus said, worried again.

"You're on the ball, all right. But I said that no

one makes the same mistake twice. The Golem was a slightly different problem. Strange things are bound to happen when you're born without a womb around you. Actually, the good Rabbi who created him used powers even we angels dare not use. So, how was I to go near him to teach him the Torah, let alone make him forget it. The Rabbi had to do all that himself. And I don't have to tell you the ultimate consequences of his efforts."

The fetus had learned about Rabbi Loew's Golem and remembered the havoc it had caused. He remembered the word the Rabbi had written on the Golem's forehead. Spastically, the fetus tried to pass his hand over his forehead to see if there were any letters or words on it. Unable to control his limbs, he accidently touched his ear. Thinking it was a letter, he kicked out in fear. This lead his mother to announce that she was going into "transition!", a state of extreme discomfort that occurs just before delivery.

The Angel saw what was happening. He realized, as he had realized so many times in the past, that God was right not to allow newborns to keep their knowledge. It was just too much for such a little thing. The sweet thoughts of a fetus could turn into nightmares with so much knowledge pressed upon its limited life experience.

"You're fine, little one," said the Angel, careful not touch his charge.

"Anyway, let me finish my original story. I

was a softie in those days. I had those rudimentary emotions that you can't flap away like a piece of cloud lint — a very annoying vestige from my human days. I should have listened to the Angel Who Teaches From Experience. She had warned me more than once to remember: An emotional Angel is a disaster waiting to happen.

"Deep down I knew it was wrong to let a fetus have its way. But this one was a strange combination of smart, subtle, cute, convincing, and logical, not unlike you, I might add. But don't get any ideas. I'm a lot smarter myself, and more experienced since those days. And, as I said, angels never make the same mistake twice.

"I gave him the Different Stages Of Development shpiel, so he would know how to behave at each stage of his babyhood. Then I explained that crying, not talking, was the way a baby entered the world. And I warned him of what kind of trouble we would get into if he didn't act like a baby when he was supposed to.

"He assured me that he understood all the rules. He also told me he knew all the stages of the development of a child, having learned it from the Torah I had taught him. And he told me something that should have warned me that I was in for a lot of grief. He told me to stop worrying."

"So what went wrong? What could possibly go wrong?" the fetus wanted to know.

"Funny, that's what I said to myself, too,"

answered the Angel. "I suppose only angels and fetuses could be so naive. Anyway, I gave him the traditional pre-flight blessing without touching his lip and whooshed him on his way.

"It was only when I heard him mumble *Tefilat HaDerech*, the traveler's prayer, as he sped down the birth canal, that I began to have misgivings. Anyway, I never reported it. I was certain that one baby out of billions couldn't make too much trouble."

"You never mentioned anything about this before," said the fetus, skeptically. "Are you sure you're not just trying to scare me?"

"Scare you? Do you think that's why I stay cooped up in here with you? To scare you?" declared the angel, highly insulted. "Do you think I would casually point out my only black dot on my otherwise pure white wings?" The angel lifted one of his wings to reveal a black dot the size of a quarter.

"Fortunately, I kept my job, but only on a technicality. The Angel For Special Souls had neglected to tell me that this little guy was a special soul. When you are dealing with a Special Soul, you get a Backup Angel to help you out, just in case you falter, like I did. The Backup Angel keeps an eye out to make sure the lip is touched before the little one is sent down the birth canal. If he sees something not kosher, well, he's got lots of ways to straighten things out.

"As it happens, The Angel For Special Souls slipped up."

"You angels seem to make mistakes rather frequently," noted the fetus.

"When you're talking about thousands and thousands of years, a mistake or two is bound to creep in," said the Angel, aware that his argument was weak.

"At the rate you Angels make mistakes, you might as well be human!" quipped the little one.

Now it was the Angel's turn to be shocked. He had never heard anything even close to sarcasm from a fetus.

"Can I please go on?" asked the Angel, curtly. He felt his vestigial emotions showing.

"Please go on," answered the fetus, meekly. He rolled up into a ball, wondering what he had said to make his Angel so upset.

His movements prompted his mother to ask why the baby had suddenly stopped moving and seemed to be rolled up in a ball. The nurse explained that this happened sometimes. No one really knew why.

"Well, if you stop playing with your umbilical cord, I'll go on," observed the Angel. He needed to feel in charge. "I've seen my share of accidents when someone decides that a belly button attachment can also be used as a lasso."

The fetus immediately let go of his umbilical cord. He had been squeezing and releasing it — a nervous habit he had developed in the womb — and now it floated above him.

"Anyway, to get back to my story, that little one slid out without incident. Everything seemed fine. I received the initial report from his Angel That Hovers Over Newborns and hear that the kid's Apgar score, you'll find out what that means soon enough — was a perfect 10. You know how it is. Out of sight, out of mind. I figured if he'd made it this far, he'd be okay.

"Besides, believe it or not, I've got a schedule to keep. Once I'm finished teaching, it's touch the top lip and move on for me. And I'm usually very business-like about it. I don't spend time reminiscing or hanging around to see what happens. Unless it's a Special Soul...." the Angel mused.

"Which reminds me of another indentation I'll never forget. Your mother and her twin."

"You did my mother?" queried the fetus.

"There's more to me than meets the eye," answered the Angel, proudly. "I like the more difficult cases, as you may have guessed by now. The Angel of Soul Management is an old friend of mine. Every now and then, he puts in a good word for me with The Angel For Special Souls and I get a very challenging case. Your mother and her brother were one of those cases."

"Does that mean you made another mistake?" suggested the fetus.

"No!" shot back the Angel.

The fetus felt the force of the Angel's anger and twisted around sharply. Afraid to grab the umbilical cord, he concentrated on getting his thumb into his mouth.

The doctor, who was checking his mother at the time, announced that the baby was rotating. "The baby's head is locked in place," he said. "I think you should start pushing," he advised.

"No mistakes," repeated the Angel, more softly this time. "But your mother and her brother hold the all time record for arguments. Arguments, argument, arguments! That's all I got from them. Your uncle tried to convince me to touch my own lip! Can you imagine that? Do you know what happens when an Angel Who Sends Forth touches his own lip? I'll tell you what happens: He has to be re-programmed by the Angel Who RePrograms Angels."

"Is that bad?" wondered the fetus. He felt a great deal of pressure and felt himself being pushed into the birth canal.

"Yes, it's very bad. When you get re-programmed you never get the same job again. Trust me on that. I used to be the Angel Who Decides The Soul's Fate until..."

"You short-circuited?" asked the fetus.

"Something like that. The truth is, I don't remember. It's a side effect of re-programming.

"But to get back to your mother and her brother. He kept arguing with me, while she twirled around just to distract me. This caused your grand-mother a great deal of concern, and indigestion.

"But you're distracting me too," realized the Angel. "I was telling you about the kid who got away."

"I want to hear about my mother," objected the fetus.

"Ask her," said the Angel. "If you remember," he added slyly.

"Before long, word came up to me that the one I let get away was standing the world on its ear. That means, creating real trouble. All that knowledge started getting to his head. That means he was too smart for his own good. People came from everywhere to hear him preach. They thought he had invented a whole new set of God's Laws, Heaven forbid.

"What he had done was sort of re-word God's Words. Lot's of human's do it. But very few have the charisma to make thousands —millions— believe that they are God's Words.

"I suppose I don't have to tell you how Moses felt. The Angel Who Serves The Great Ones reported that Moses almost decided to return to the world. He wanted to confront the troublemaker. Couldn't really blame him. So much good work being reinterpreted. The Angel Who Serves The Great Ones was beside himself. Of course, I was called in and well, what could I say? Lamely, I tried to explain what happened."

"Was everyone very angry with you?" asked the fetus. The sack of fluid he was in was contracting, pushing him downward.

"I'm just fortunate that Moses didn't press charges against me. I came very close to becoming the new Angel Who Sweeps Up. But, true to form, Moses prayed for me, and, well, the rest is history, which you will find out soon enough.

"As a matter of fact, I think the time has come for you to find out right now. So stop twirling and give me your lip."

"No," said the fetus, adamantly. "I want to know what happened to the other fetus. Did he become great?"

"He became great, all right," admitted the Angel. "The whole world soon heard about him. A new religion grew up around him. But the world went through some very difficult times because of him. Years later, the people Moses had led out of the wilderness suffered for a while because of that religion."

The fetus began to think. The pressure on his head was powerful. He was afraid and curious and anxious, all at the same time.

"Maybe I could fix things up?" he suggested. "Maybe I can convince the people that Moses was right?"

The Angel smiled.

"Nice try. But I'm not making the same, er, misjudgment, twice. And anyway, feel that pres-

**95**

sure? Your mother is in the final stages of labor. You're going to be pushed out of here soon. So, give me your lip."

"What if I refuse?" asked the fetus, showing more daring than he really felt.

"That's your choice," confided the Angel. "But it's my choice to let you go into the world alive." The Angel let his words sink in.

"Without touching your lip, I can't complete my job, and I'll have no choice.... So, let me have your lip."

At that moment, the fetus felt the strongest pressure yet. He knew that the time for birth was at hand. He had no choice.

The fetus leaned his head forward, watching the Angel's hand reach for his lip. But the fetus couldn't help himself. At the last moment, he lifted his head up high. The Angel's finger burned into his lower lip. The fetus felt a slight tingle, but nothing more.

"There, doesn't that feel better?" asked the Angel, still unaware of what had happened. "Goodbye."

The fetus felt himself being pushed out of his mother's womb. In keeping with the Torah he had learned, the fetus said the traveler's prayer and then began the birthing process.

"Stop him!" shouted the Backup Angel. "You touched the wrong lip!"

But it was too late.

"You've sent another fetus forth without touching his lip!" scolded the Angel For Special Souls.

The Angel Who Sends Forth was wingbroken. He knew this would be the end of his career. This was such a bad mistake that even Moses would not be able to help him. Not this time.

The Angel Who Sends Forth gazed back at his wings. He was waiting to see how much black would spread across his wings. He watched the black dot. But instead of enlarging, the black dot began to disappear, until his wings were pure white, something he had not seen for 2,000 years.

"Well done!" a voice announced. The Angel Who Sends Forth quickly realized that this was not another angel talking. "It has taken you 2,000 years, but at last you have corrected your mistake."

"It is time for the Messiah to arrive," announced God. "Now Moses, and all the people of the world, will know My Glory.

"And you, Angel Who Sends Forth, you will no longer be called Angel Who Sends Forth. From now on, you will be called Angel Who Stands At God's Right Hand."

This was more than the Angel could handle. He had gone from the depths of despair to the heights of Godliness. He was to stand at the right hand of God.

"What will be my job?" asked the Angel Who Stands At God's Right Hand.

"Your job," answered God, "will be to watch over my chosen one — for ever and ever."

So, dear reader, if, as a child, you feel the urge to confront people with the wonderful, God-inspired news that "A New Day Is Coming!" you would do well to check your lip — not the upper one, the lower lip.

Go ahead. Do it.

Do you notice an indentation just below the middle part of your lower lip? Yes?

Well, then let me be the first to congratulate you: You've arrived!

Halleluyah!

# My Clone and I

by Miriam Biskin

MIRIAM BISKIN enjoys life. Her plays, stories, and poems have been published in *The New York Times*, *Jack and Jill*, and many children's magazines.

Miriam likes keeping up with current scientific research (although she likes golf more). Leave it to her to find a new solution to the age-old problem of having to practice for your Bar/Bat mitzvah. Of course, sometimes you can have *two* much of a good thing....

At eight, I, Adam Mordecai Goldstein, was a high school class valedictorian. At nine, I was inducted into MENSA; at eleven, I was working on my doctorate in Bio-Technological Engineering; and as my twelfth birthday approached, I was contemplating my Post-Doctoral thesis in Reprogenetics. It was about that time that I began to hear about other plans my father and mother were making for my Bar Mitzvah. I couldn't believe that they actually took my involvement with such an archaic tradition for granted, and I was amazed that the Rabbi was adamant that I attend classes and private sessions with him to discuss my Torah portion.

"Rabbi Weiss," I protested, "you know that I am already fluent in the classical languages, Latin, Greek, Sanskrit, and Hebrew as well." I modestly omitted the fact that I also had proficiency in French, Russian, Spanish, Japanese, Swedish, and Swahili, to mention just a few.

"But my studies...my research," I stammered. "I don't have the time."

"It is written," he said, "that the study of Torah exceeds all."

It was obvious that he wasn't going to budge.

At home my father shrugged. "It's your decision," he said, which is about the worst thing a parent can say.

Mom was holding her mouth in a tight line.

Grandfather's eyes were filled with tears.

Grandmother was already wiping her wet cheeks.

I couldn't face my mother and father's disappointment and my grandparents' sorrow, so I acquiesced.

"You make us proud," my grandfather said, patting my cheek.

"We love you so," added Grandma, hugging me close.

For just a moment, I felt a twinge of guilt, but it passed as I became focused on my own plan.

It was easy. I like to do research at odd hours, so I have my own key to the Genetic Enhancement Clinic and to the cryo-preservation storage area where units are stored at a temperature of minus 96 degrees Celsius.

It's been a long time since the arrival of Dolly the Sheep and her brood first astonished the world, and the techniques used by those researchers and breeders trying to split embryos into beings with the exact same genetic information are now pathetically outdated. Only historic scientific journals discuss the procedures whereby sperm cells and mature egg cells were gathered in petri dishes to produce offspring.

"Uncertain and messy," is how my mentor, Dr. Bokanovsky, describes these protocols. His technique is based on analytical chemistry, involving the breaking down of any specimen into its component parts and then reconstructing a programmed entity which grows spontaneously.

The animal collection goes from aardvark to zebra, with the same wide selections of fish and fowl, created with such expertise the ecologists no longer worry about certain species becoming extinct. However, despite all of this scientific progress, the moral and legal rights of human entities are still constantly debated, and replications are available only by court order in certain unique circumstances. For me, legal recourse was no solution, since a request for a reprieve from the Bar Mitzvah rigamarole would be thrown out of court. Nevertheless, Clone kits were being produced in anticipation of federal approval. With my top level security clearance, I would have no problem gaining entry to the GEC.

The only person on duty at the clinic was the security guard who nodded in recognition as I let myself into the cryogenic lab. The crib areas were labeled by species, with display and dispensing areas much like some 20th century candy vending machines. All I had to do was encode my student identification card, make my selection, and wait for the appropriate packet to drop into the receiving pocket. It was thermal wrapped and small enough for me to stash in my back pack and leave without arousing the guard's suspicions.

In the privacy of my bedroom I read the directions which were a bit more complicated than I had anticipated. Without any of the lab's sophisticated equipment, I had to improvise. Working with thermal mitts, I unpacked the freeze-dried parts one by one, laid them on the floor on a large towel, and began to reassemble them like a jigsaw puzzle. Then, using a computer-generated probe, hooked by relay into the lab laser generator, I scanned in my most recent photograph to churn out a real-life simulation of myself. Since copies are always less defined than the original, I knew that some faculties would be lacking, but my new self was good enough to escape detection. The last directive involved the submersion of the replica in warm water, partially to step up the thawing process and also to allow the ingestion of the appropriate amount of water.

Within moments, the thawing was complete and his arms and legs began to flop around. Hair grew in appropriate places. And, as he opened his eyes, I watched as my reasonable facsimile rose from the tub and began toweling off.

"Usually, I take showers," he said.

"Yeah," I said, "usually you do."

"I must have been feeling cold," he said.

*"I unpacked the freeze-dried parts one by one...."*

"Hand me my robe, will you? It's on that hook behind that door."

Amazed, I did as he requested. He was really right at home.

"Who are you?" he asked.

"I'm Adam," I said.

"Me, too," he laughed. "That's funny.

Thus I named him . . . ME2.

"I'm still a little cold," he said. "And I'm very tired."

Before I knew it, a twelve-year-old boy had moved into my bedroom, thrown himself across the bed, and had his head on my pillow. As I threw a blanket over him, he opened his eyes and murmured, "Thanks."

"Oh, go to sleep," I whispered, a bit put off by his taking over so easily.

"Goodnight," he said agreeably and began to snore lightly. Somehow, I managed to push him over to make a place for myself, and I drifted off, too.

Early next morning, I was awakened by voices outside my door.

"Sweetheart," my mother saying. "You look so rested. You slept well?"

"Like a baby," he (or I should say I) responded.

"Are you hungry, sweetheart?" she asked. "I made pancakes."

"I'm starved," he said, "and nobody makes pancakes like my mom."

Mom giggled. "You are so sweet today. I though you might still be annoyed with us."

It took a while for him to finish breakfast, and when he came back up to the bedroom, I saw he was  dressed in old  jeans and my high school sweatshirt, things that I would like to wear to work, but seldom do. It was already late, and I was tired from the previous night so I decided to let him go off to the  lab in my place.

"What do I have to do today?" he asked

"Just sit at the desk and look smart," I instructed.

" I guess I can do that," he agreed, lauging.

Content, I went back to bed. When I awoke, it was after five, and just as I was beginning to get concerned, he sauntered in.

"Where were you?" I asked.

"I got tired of sitting at the desk, and then some of the guys asked me to play cards with them.

It sounded like fun."

"Cards?"

"Yeah...they called it *Twenty-one*. The dealer puts two cards down and deals two. Then you ask for another card and whoever gets closest to 21 wins."

"I know all about it, but I don't gamble."

"I wasn't gambling. *They* were betting on me because I'm so good at figuring odds."

"You mean probabilities. How did you do?"

"Great. Only the other guys we played against said we were cheating."

I felt disgusted. How could I face my colleagues and explain that I had been duped into using my mathematical skills for monetary advantage? I really couldn't blame ME2. After all, it was his first day on the job.

The next morning, I got up before he did and went to ask the Dean for a leave of absence to study for my Bar Mitzvah. He was most understanding.

"Even for such a short time, academia will feel your loss," he told me. "But I am proud of you for honoring your people's traditions."

He guaranteed that my experimental data and my lab would be locked up until my return, which fit in perfectly with my plans. Since my lab was essentially off-limits to everyone, I could spend as much time as I liked working there. There was an old cot which I could sleep on, and I could sneak food out of the commissary. In that way, ME2 could spend his time at home, and our paths never had to cross.

Later, when ME2 was taking a nap, I told my parents about my Bar Mitzvah plans.

"What did the Dean say?" my father asked.

"He said that he thought that the time off would do me good," I answered, making a quick retreat before ME2 could come downstairs.

Later, when everyone was at dinner, I took the opportunity to gather my stuff and sneak out the back door, but not before I eavesdropped on a bit of the table conversation.

"Since you have some free time now," Dad was saying, "how would you like to help me in the store?"

"Sure," answered ME2. "How's tomorrow?"

I had so many fond memories of being in Dad's sporting goods store when I was a little fellow that I almost envied ME2. I used to love wandering up and down the aisles, swinging baseball bats and dribbling basketballs.

Each clone kit comes with a Sensitizer which allows you to tune into your clone's activities. I used it the next day to keep tabs on my double image.

ME2 spent most of the day whistling happily as he put aerobikes together.

"How come I don't have one of these?" he asked my father.

"You said you never had the time to ride one."

"I'd like one now," he said.

Dad laughed. "Then pick one out. We'll call it a pre-Bar Mitzvah present."

ME2 picked out exactly the one I would have taken, and soon he was airbiking along on his way to the Rabbi's house.

I reset my coordinates so that I could follow him a bit further.

"I think I'm early," I heard him say to the Rabbi.

"Never too early to cultivate the Jewish spirit...come in and make yourself comfortable."

Then as ME2 munched on some cookies, we both settled down to hear what the Rabbi was going to say.

"The most important ambition that anyone can have in life, Adam," said the Rabbi, "is to be a complete *mensch*. To study and to learn is important, but equally important is the willingness to share what you know."

Then he began to tell stories of great Jewish scientists who worked not for profit or fame, but to make the lives of others better. Schick, Salk...the list was endless. They were the models that he wanted ME2 to follow.

Each day the Rabbi explored a new topic, and I rarely missed a session. Things went along smoothly.... ME2 got along famously with the Rabbi.

"He teaches me so much," he would say to my parents. "I come away feeling happy and fulfilled after each session."

Then he would tell over the lesson for that day.

One afternoon, as ME2 sat with the Rabbi discussing acts of loving kindness, he became very thoughtful.

"Is there something I can do?" he asked.

"You have started on the path, by accepting your obligation to be a Bar Mitzvah."

"But I did that for me," said ME2.

"I thought it was for your parents and grandparents."

"That was then...now it's for me."

"If I am not for myself," said the Rabbi, quoting from Hillel, "then who will be for me?"

"I'm glad you're enjoying the experience. But now I have another project for you. Since you have the time and the talent, I would consider it a favor if you would help Sammy Cohen for a few hours a week with his Jewish History."

ME2 agreed.

Because Sammy was a bit slow at remembering events, ME2 designed a visual-reality program which served as a time machine, taking

Sammy through all of the historic places in Israel. When he touched down on a particular place, the machine would visually highlight all the events in Jewish history that had happened in that place. The animated characters ME2 created were so life-like, and the action scenes so realistic that on more than one occasion Sammy actually asked the characters questions, which of course ME2 quickly answered. It was so fascinating that I often went along for the "ride."

"Sammy's grasp of history has certainly improved," said the Rabbi to ME2. "He's become positively excited about his heritage. You are a born teacher."

Then, using electronic flash cards which replicated both the look and sound of Hebrew words and phrases, ME2 began to work on Sammy's Hebrew vocabulary. As items appeared on the small screen, a voice intoned the Hebrew pronunciation of the word. ME2 and Sammy repeated each word. I tuned in as I sat at my lab desk, unconsciously chiming in. ME2 even worked it out so that concepts and abstract words could be displayed on the screen in the form of visual examples which made it easier to remember the word in Hebrew. It was a work of genius.

At the Rabbi's suggestion, ME2 and Sammy began to undertake specific acts of loving kindness. They collected canned good for the local food drive and helped collect discarded items for a rummage sale. They spent afternoons in the Home for the Aged visiting with people who rarely had visitors. They went to the hospital with the Rabbi as he comforted the sick and even to houses where people were sitting *shiva*, where they offered consolation to those in mourning.

The days wore on and ME2 did more and more acts of loving kindness. I was a little worried that perhaps he was doing too much. He often seemed tired and had begun to take regular daily naps.

Occasionally, when he was asleep, I would sneak back into the house to check on things. On the rare occasion when I ran into one of my parents, they apparently saw no difference between us. But my Mom couldn't help but comment how well I looked whenever she saw me, and how pale my double looked when she met him.

I made it my business to listen in each day as he came home from his lessons with the Rabbi. The truth is, I was beginning to enjoy not only the lessons, but the daily exchange he would have with my mother.

"How was it today, Adam?" Mom would ask.

"Just fine," he would answer.

"Are you tired after all that study?"

"No, it's fun."

"It is so wonderful," she would say. "Every time I see the Rabbi, he tells me how you've matured, and how proud he is of how fast you are progressing."

Then, one day, ME2 told my mother he was learning how to sing our portion of the Torah reading.

"We're starting to learn the *trop*," he said.

"Oh, Grandpa would love to help you learn the melodies. He knows them all and he has a wonderful voice."

"Would you ask him?" ME2 requested.

"Ask? It would be his pleasure."

The thought of MY Grandfather working with ME2 didn't please me that much, but I guess this was the way things had to be.

"And maybe after dinner, you can help me pick out the invitations and the *yarmulkas*."

"Sure. What's for dinner, Mom?"

"Your favorite, baked chicken with roasted potatoes."

I began to salivate. That was MY favorite dinner. Part of the price I had to pay in this deception was eating the lab commissary food.

As the time drew near, It was obvious that ME2 was growing nervous.

"Keep this up and you'll be getting gray before your time," laughed Dad.

"He's been doing too much," said Mom.

Even with reassurances from them and from Grandpa and the Rabbi, he was still tense. Mom tried to keep him busy, making decisions about the florist and the caterer and all the other minute details, while Dad sought his advice on which members of the family might take parts in the service. I was glad that ME2, and not me, was the one going through all this.

The big day arrived, and friends and relatives began to fill the synagogue. ME2 looked fine in his new navy suit and tie, wearing one of the navy blue yarmulkas he had chosen with Mom. He was hugged by uncles and aunts and assorted relatives who threw compliments at him from all sides.

"How handsome you look!"

"How tall you have grown!"

I sat unobtrusively in the back of the synagogue, and as the Sabbath service began, a sense of peace came over me. I was proud watching myself (or rather, ME2) seated in the big chair alongside the Rabbi on the *bimah*.

The service progressed, and as he stepped up to the podium, ME2 seemed poised and suddenly older.

The *gabayim* unrolled the Torah scroll, and a name was called for the first *aliyah*.

"Meyer Itzah ben Naphtali haCohane...."

Grandpa, wearing a yarmulka and a prayer shawl, got up from his seat and took his place next to ME2.

Smiling with pride to be part of his grandson's big day, grandpa put a hand on ME2's shoulder as he began to read from the scroll.

"There's a proud and happy man if I've ever seen one," said someone who had taken a seat beside me. It was Dr. Bonkovansky!

"If you're watching the Bar Mitzvah boy," he said, "you'll begin to notice that he is starting to look tired. I doubt he will be able to finish the Torah reading. When you created him you should have checked his expiration date."

Sure enough, even as I watched, ME2 began growing pale. I didn't know what to do. I turned to face my mentor, but Dr.B. was already walking toward the bimah, speaking above the weakening voice of ME2. I could hear him saying something about the boy being ill and about being a physician and suggesting a few moments recess. With that, he took ME2 by the hand and led him to the back of the synagogue. Then he motioned for me to help him. I could see that ME2 was shivering and when I came over and held him, his hands were ice-cold.

We took him to one of the classrooms that lined the hall leading into the synagogue proper. Dr.B. quickly locked the door behind us.

"Take his jacket," he commanded.

"He's sick," I protested. "He needs it."

"Don't worry," he countered. "He can have mine, and I have a thermal suit in this bag."

I hadn't even noticed the bag Dr.B. was

carrying. Swiftly, he took a thermal suit from out of it and began dressing ME2.

"What can I do to help?" I asked.

"You can go out there and finish what you started," he advised.

ME2 smiled weakly. "Hurry," he urged.

Dr.B. unlocked the door and pushed me through it. There was small burst of applause as I walked back to my place.

"Feel better?" asked the Rabbi. "I see you changed ties," he added.

I had worn the same suit as ME2 but I hadn't thought to wear the same tie.

"It's my lucky tie," I ad-libed.

I began to read. Every word, every syllable flowed into place. After listening to ME2 practice so long, I had learned our Torah reading to perfection. My Haftorah reading went just as smoothly.

After the accolades, the Rabbi asked me to address the congregations. It was time for my *d'var Torah*.

My hands shook as I read ME2's speech. I thanked everyone for sharing this great occasion in my life, for all the gifts of love and kindness I had been given. I read his words about the marvel of giving and the wonder of receiving, and when he quoted the Rabbi's saying that the highest level of charity was to help someone help himself, I realized what ME2 had done for me.

In spite of the gala spirit during the rest of the day and the evening, I couldn't get ME2 out of my mind. After the Sabbath, I tried calling Dr.B. at his home and at his office, but there was no reply.

The next morning, even though it was Sunday, I made some excuse to leave the house and went back to the lab.

Everything was just as I had left it, except for a memo from Dr.B. which read "SEE ME, A.S.A.P."

Fearfully, I knocked on his door, aware of the fact that I WAS guilty of several scientific and legal infractions. Secretly, I hoped he was not in.

"Come in," a voice ordered.

"You wanted to see me, sir?" I asked, poking my head into his office.

"Yes, I did. Come in, Adam." He waited until I was seated.

"I am disappointed in you, Adam," he began. "You should have been more thorough. You, better than anyone else, know that it is the little details which help us succeed, both in life and in creating life. You should have checked the kit and noted his expiration date."

"I didn't mean any harm, sir," I whispered. "I am so sorry. Is he...dead?"

"He almost was. Fortunately, I got him to the rejuvenation vats on time. "

"Good," was all I could manage.

There was another knock on the door.

"Ah, that must be your new mentor," said Dr. B. "I knew you would come in today and I wanted to introduce you."

With that, a gray-haired gentleman walked into the room. He could have been my father or my grandfather. There was something so familiar about him.

"Come in," said Dr.B. to the newcomer. "I want you to meet Adam Goldstein."

"How strange," said the man with a friendly smile. "My name is Adam, too."

# Medizinmann

*by Dan Pearlman*

DAN PEARLMAN teaches Creative Writing at the University of Rhode Island. His stories have appeared in Amazing Stories and SF Anthologies, and his novels have a distinct twist to them.

In this supernatural story, a shtetl magician calls upon a host of not-always-heavenly beings to rain judgment upon a group of soldiers who have lost more than their way....

Thc sputter of a motorcycle interrupted the colonel's reflections on Wagner's Gutterdammerung. His head did not budge; his eyes remained fixed, through the windshield of his newly-captured American-made jeep, on the metal fortress rolling along in front of him. Of his three remaining tanks, the Tiger rumbled slowly over the frozen rutted road keeping a hundred meters ahead of him. From the top of the tank, a crewman scanned the patchy forest through binoculars, watchful also of the ragtag procession of infantry and trucks behind. Two Panzers brought up the rear, but for several days now the massive Russian onslaught had ignored Colonel Knatte's limping unit.

Had he made a wrong turn, he wondered, in the smoke and confusion of the last air attack? Or were the other units crawling ahead faster than his? All that he had each day to remind him that he was still in the midst of a war was the far-off, sporadic thunder of bombs and artillery shelling. By now he should have run into some other regimental stragglers. The prolonged isolation worried him, but the last idea he would accept was that he was "lost."

Although alone, he was moving west and enjoying a holiday from further bombardment. The road was passable, and snow had ceased falling for days. There was grumbling among the troops about losing touch with their brigade (whatever was left of it), but at least they had to thank him for this respite from battle, for this welcome stretch of time to lick their wounds. Rations would last for six days more, fuel for eight (unless temperatures again fell to the point at which the tanks had to be kept idling all night to prevent them from freezing!). Surely, long before their fuel gave out, they were bound to be absorbed into the main body of the retreat. All this would have been enough to muffle his nagging anxieties, if he didn't also have Von Steinhausen on his back.

Colonel Knatte did not want to turn and look at the motorcycle coming up on the left. It was another twitching fragment of a proud thing that once had been a squadron. The isolated unit had been cut down again—to the strength of barely a company—after a strafing five days earlier by a lone Soviet fighter, a stray flea hopping off the Russian bear's back. A plane made of wood! A toy that would have been blown out of the skies by the tailwind alone of a JU52 — before the Luftwaffe committed suicide at Stalingrad (under orders from Der Fuhrer, of course).

"What is it now?" came a weak, raspy voice

from the back of the jeep.

The colonel tossed a glance over his left shoulder at the blanket-wrapped form of his special charge, his "protege," who lay uncomfortably splayed over the whole of the back seat, his head propped up on rags that doubled as polishing cloths. The canvas-topped jeep with intact side curtains had no doubt belonged to an officer, thought the colonel. The canvas kept out the freezing wind, yet the captain had begun to shiver.

"You are awake, Hauptmann Von Steinhausen? Have you had much rest this morning?"

"Not very much, Herr Oberst."

"How are you feeling, Captain?"

"Not particularly good, Herr Oberst. Perhaps we are about to hear some news. Perhaps we've made radio contact with the rest of the brigade."

"Have patience! It won't be much longer before we run into a unit with proper medical facilities."

"With someone who can saw off my leg."

"We must not assume that such drastic measures will be necessary, Captain." On and off, for two days now, Von Steinhausen had been having bouts of delirium. This was one of his rarer moments of lucidity. He had refused to be dumped among the close-packed wounded in the only truck left that had room for them. Knatte had obliged, bundling him up and stashing him in the back of the jeep by himself.

"My father will be happy if you get me back

in one piece, even if slightly foreshortened."

"The general placed complete confidence in me, and I do not intend to disappoint him."

"If you get me back alive, no matter what parts are missing, he will still be sure to angle you a promotion."

"My career is the last thing on my mind, Captain Von Steinhausen!" The impertinence of the pup! He was sure that if the captain were in full possession of his faculties he would have spoken more tactfully in the presence of the driver. Promotion was not on Knatte's mind. The destruction of his career was more likely if Von Steinhausen were to die. The general had dropped a broad hint to that effect. And the captain's death seemed so imminent a possibility—the gangrene seemed so advanced—that Colonel Knatte was willing to try anything to save him.

He did not like how close alongside the jeep the motorcyclist had managed to position himself. All that he had left between himself and dignity was this Ford-built jeep, captured several months ago from the American-supplied Russians, when Moscow had not seemed so very far away. A sturdy substitute for the Horch 40 command car he had lost two bombings ago, the olive-drab jeep had become a shining testament to his pride of leadership in adversity. His driver cleaned it up for him each morning and during each break in the exhausting march westward.

The colonel had the hood waxed and then

polished to such a high gloss that he boasted he could use it to shave by. This polishing, he would freely admit, was a magical sort of ritual—a fanciful attempt to reverse the flow of time so that the army was not engaged in "retreat" but was returning to its pristine strength and hope, as if wound up inside a film that was being run backward....

The motorcycle teetered within a scratch of the fender.

The colonel pushed back his side curtain. "What the hell do you think you're doing?" he shouted.

"I'm sorry, Herr Oberst. I have no intention of grazing your jeep." The cyclist veered off slightly, skillfully maneuvering the ridges and gullies in front of him. "The peasant we picked up an hour ago has been interrogated. He claims he knows of someone who can help our wounded."

"A local physician?"

"He calls him a healer, sir."

"Some peasant herbalist?"

"No. Some sort of...magician, sir."

"Magician! Is this some sort of a joke, Obergefreite Weiss?"

"The man swears by him, Colonel, sir."

"If he has good boots, make sure you remove them after you have him shot."

"Jawohl, Herr Oberst."

"Wait," said Captain Von Steinhausen, almost

inaudibly. "Sometimes country healers are better than the best medical specialists in Berlin."

The colonel thought for a moment. A shaman! A Medizinmann! It was grasping at a straw, but what could he lose by trying—except valuable time and some fuel? He had much more to lose, in fact, if he did not explore even the remotest possibility. Such neglect would not sit well with the general. "All right, Corporal Weiss. Where do we find this magic Russian?"

The corporal waved his arm to the right. "In a little village about ten kilometers north, through the woods."

Ten kilometers was stretching it! "All right, Corporal. I will talk to your peasant about this native Russian healer."

The motorcycle took a serious jolt, but the rider recovered his balance. "This healer is not a ... native Russian, sir."

"No? What then, a gypsy?"

"He says he is a Jew, sir."

"A Jew! Is there a Jew left alive in this part of Russia? I thought the Einsatzgruppen prided themselves on their thoroughness."

"Before the Fuhrer, our family physician was a Jew, Colonel Knatte," said the captain. "I'm sure my father won't take it amiss if we tried."

The colonel stroked his chin for a while, then ordered his driver to signal to the tank crewman ahead of him. They would set up camp in the woods. The troops had been moving since dawn; they could use a break. "I would not doubt," said the colonel, "that a Jew with some knowledge of medicine might be regarded by a muzhik as a magician."

Reb Yoel Sternberg was surprised by the knock at the door—the outside door of the shed he had built onto his house. Was Rabbi Dovidl so impatient for him to repair the synagogue bench that he had sent out one of the old men into the cold late-morning wind, out to the edge of the village, just to see how Mr. Fix-it was doing? Whoever was out in that wailing wind had to be dying to get into the shed! The large stove in the house served also to heat the shed, through a metal duct he had built—to the awe of every hassid in the village.

Reb Yoel was distrustful of the silence following the knock. "Who is it?" he called. No one answered. He called to his wife through the closed door that communicated with the kitchen. "Rivka?" Again, no answer. No answer from Rivkele?

Taking no chances, he snatched up a hammer from the fender of his old truck. Before the war the old pick-up had earned him his livelihood, but now, long useless from the lack of fuel, it had rusted away and served only as a storage bin for scraps of anything a handyman could salvage from a world that had collapsed around his ears.

Reb Yoel slid back the bolt and opened the door a few inches. "Fedka!"

It was Fyodor Vasilievich, for years the village shabbos goy, chopping firewood and heating the stove for the synagogue on the Sabbath. Four or five years ago, on the death of his wife, Fedka had moved in with a widowed sister in the distant town of Krichev. "Come in, Fedka. What brings you back to our miserable, Godforsaken Drozh?"

"Forgive me, Rabbi Yoel." Bundled up in a ragged coat unfit for a horse, Fedka spread his palms in the air. "I was in a work crew which the Germans broke up when they began moving back in the opposite—" Suddenly the door sprung open and the peasant, shoved forward, dropped face-down in the shed.

"*Lass das, Jude!*" The German sergeant, brandishing a submachine gun, nodded at Reb Yoel's hammer. Numb with terror, he dropped it. A smart-looking officer now elbowed aside the soldier and stepped through the doorway, taking in everything at a glance.

"You are Yoel Sternberg the healer, are you not?" said the officer in German.

"The people around here call me so, yes, Colonel," said Yoel.

"Herr Oberst!", the Colonel corrected.

"Yes, Herr Oberst," Yoel repeated

"And take off your cap when you talk to me, Jew."

"Sorry, Herr Oberst," said Yoel, slipping his fur cap under his arm.

"You recognize my rank and you speak with a Viennese accent. Where are you from and what are you doing out here?" At a signal from the colonel, the sergeant stepped in and shut the door behind him. Fedka rose warily to his feet.

"I left Vienna just before the Anschluss, sir. My good Viennese neighbors, whom I had often helped when their physicians had given up on them, began accusing me of practicing medicine without a license—even of witchcraft, believe it or not!" Reb Yoel tried a broad smile, but the Nazi officer's glare failed to change. "I picked out this little hassidic village because it was nowhere, because I wanted to get lost, because no real doctor would ever set foot in a miserable hole like Drozh. And because the rabbi needed a handyman."

"You and your entire village could be shot for harboring this truck, you know," said the colonel, threateningly.

"We could be shot just for existing, sir, but why for a truck that has not run for years?"

The colonel looked at the truck and gave the flattened rear tire a dismissive kick. "This peasant says you cured both his wife and his cow of severe illnesses that each contracted after expelling their respective litters. Is this true?"

"I don't like to take credit for it personally," said Yoel. Shrugging his shoulders, he glanced down at the colonel's polished boots below the hem of his thick woolen overcoat. "These hands, somehow, are able to serve as a lens through which certain *forces*, let's call them, whether natural or supernatural—"

"Yes, yes, I know there must be some explanation. Frankly, I don't care if the devil himself lends a hand.... And explain to me this nonsense about making it rain! Your peasant here claims that you were able to end a drought that threatened the local farmers with complete loss of their crops. Is that why you are also known as a magician?"

Reb Yoel threw out his palms. "What do you expect of ignorant peasants, Colonel, sir? They begged me to devise some sort of a rain-making ceremony. I did everything I could to get out of it, you know. I threatened them that the devil could be listening, and that if the Evil One decided to give them rain, he might take a few lives in payment. 'That's all right with us,' they said. Desperate, you know. Well, the fact that it did rain—"

"—was pure coincidence, naturally," the colonel interjected, "but your peasants were particularly impressed by the death of three of their elders as soon as your week-long downpour was over."

"There's a price for everything. But I've never liked people calling me a *magician*," lamented Yoel, shaking his head.

"I don't give a damn what you are, Sternberg. A member of my staff received a shrapnel wound to the right lower leg that now looks badly gangrenous. At the moment we have inadequate medical services. If you can help him, I will forget I ever saw you and your village."

"And if not, Herr Oberst?"

"Your fellow villagers have all been placed under guard at your synagogue, Sternberg. If I were you, I would think positively."

"The act of healing requires a communal ceremony," said Yoel, trying desperately to cloak the tremor in his voice. "The only place large enough for us all to assemble, and which is reasonably well heated, is the synagogue."

"We found a good many of the older men gathered there already. And apart from their wives, there weren't too many others available to round up. Where are all the young people, Sternberg?"

"You came upon a village dying of old age, sir. I'm about the youngest left, and I'm in my forties. Our youth have either been drafted into the army, or have drifted away to more prosperous towns." Could the colonel see in his eyes that he was lying? Reb Yoel looked away. He had told him exactly the same story that the old folks at the synagogue would have told him. If the colonel came to suspect the truth, that the majority of the young had joined the ranks of the partisans, no one in the village would be spared, thought Yoel, whether his *medical* services proved efficacious or not.

"You will ride with us then to your synagogue. Come and sit with Captain Von Steinhausen in the jeep. He is the officer you are to treat."

"My wife—"

"She has been taken to the synagogue. Go and put your coat on, quick!" The colonel turned around to his companion. "Sergeant Gerhardt, take the peasant outside and dispose of him."

On hearing the colonel's order, Reb Yoel was unable to move. If to save his old friend he could have summoned all the demons out of hell, no matter the consequences.... He started mumbling a prayer, the Shema. A shove in the back sent him stumbling toward his overcoat, which hung, like the corpse of a bear, from a hook beside the workbench.

The trip to the shul was wordless. The pallid captain was unconscious. The colonel had arranged him in the back of the jeep to make a bit of room for

Yoel. Sergeant Gerhardt drove across the plank bridge toward the village center and the synagogue, a building made of wood and the only two-story structure in Drozh. Near the entrance stood a canvas-backed truck. A pair of helmeted sentries guarded the synagogue doors.

Yoel entered first, to the left of the great tiled stove that spread its warmth through the one-room interior. The place reeked of wax, of burnt potatoes, and of mildewed books. It smelt of something else, too, the terror of the 70 or so villagers huddled there, standing among the study tables and benches. They were being watched from below by two soldiers with rifles, and from above by a machine-gunner in the balcony reserved for women. The name "Reb Yoel" echoed through the hall.

"Silence!" snapped one of the guards. "Get back!" He blocked the path of a black-haired woman with trim, regular features in a ghostly-pale face.

"Rivka!"

"Thank God you're safe, Yoel!"

"My services are being called upon, Rivka." His wife looked embarrassed to be standing amidst the men, in defiance of Orthodox custom. Reluctantly, she backed off to rejoin the women who stood clustered against the rear wall.

Yoel turned to the colonel. "We must place the captain on the floor here, in front of the stove." The colonel ordered one of the outside sentries to help Sergeant Gerhardt carry the officer in. They laid the half-conscious, muttering Von Steinhausen on a blanket in the floor-space indicated.

"This is what you have to contend with, Sternberg." The colonel exposed the infected leg, unwinding cloths that had been wrapped loosely around it from the toes up to well above the knee. Yoel examined the dark, mottled flesh, part bloated, part shriveled, that extended out from the calf-wound sending long red tendrils far up onto the bleached, shrunken thigh. He reached his hands out toward the wretched-looking limb, anticipating the power-surge that would ripple through his fingers...if all went well.

"What do you think?" said the colonel.

"It is an advanced case. But with God's help...."

"Yes or no, Sternberg? Is there anything you can do?"

"I need their support, their energy," said Yoel, glancing around at all the grim faces, at the dozens of pairs of eyes that hung on his every movement. "May I reassure them that you mean them no harm?"

"Go ahead and reassure them."

"May I tell them that you permit them to relax and sit down?"

"Say whatever is necessary," said the colonel.

"You have permission to be seated," said Reb Yoel in Yiddish, motioning at the crowd with his palms. "Let the rebbe take his seat beside the Ark." He watched as Rabbi Dovidl, a very old man with a long white beard, was led—forced, really, muttering and shaking his fist—to a seat along the left-hand wall opposite the central platform from which he normally conducted prayer services. It had taken years until the town's hassidic rebbe had come to trust this Ashkenazi newcomer, this German-Jewish healer, whom he had at first suspected of wanting to usurp his authority. (He still did not address Yoel by the honorific "Reb" accorded men of recognized stature in the community.)

"The colonel seeks our help in curing this young officer of a severely infected limb. In return for our assistance, he assures me that we will all be left in peace." The room broke out in murmurs and muffled cries.

"And what happens, Yoel, if you do not succeed?" came the rabbi's booming voice, belying his frailty of body. Women began to wail. Old men in skullcaps and long black capotehs shifted and shuffled about in confusion. The alarmed soldiers looked toward the colonel, who signaled his minions to relax.

"With everybody's help, I will succeed! I ask you all to concentrate, to picture this man's limb restored to its former condition."

As Reb Yoel began his incantations, a thousand voices filled his ears, coming from distant fields and woods, muttering, protesting. Gritting his teeth, he ignored them and flashed an awkward grin at the colonel. "I must beg your indulgence, Herr Oberst. The ceremony includes things that an educated man must regard as...hocus pocus."

"Hocus pocus?"

"Oh, you know, things that will sound like mumbo-jumbo, abracadabra. Magical spells and such. We want to summon the appropriate spirits and keep at arm's length all others."

"Yes. Creating a mood. Good psychology, Sternberg."

Reb Yoel laughed with embarrassment. After taking a saltshaker off the table in front of the stove, he walked three times around the moribund captain, leaving a circle of salt grains in his path. Three times he intoned the charm against the fever demon, one of many formulae learned at his mother's knee: "Ochnotinos, chnotinos, notinos, otinos, tinos, inos, nos, os." As the demon's name shrunk letter by letter, so too did his power.

And then Reb Yoel entered the charmed circle, got to his knees, and made passes with his palms, back and forth over the length of the ravaged limb. Never did he have to touch the skin, sensing, as a result of long practice, the proper distance to cruise above the body. Soon he felt the heat-flush in his hands, the beginning of the process, the initial contribution of energy, which always had to come from himself.

But at the same time he maintained, uninterrupted, a stream of incantations in Hebrew, now invoking the Shechina, the presence of God Himself; and now, out of His host of deputy angels, the Princes of Healing — Metatron, and Shaddai, and Sandalfon; bidding the angel Dumah keep a lock on the realm of the dead and forbid the awakening of the angels of destruction, those dread, keen-scented malah, kabbal, who would "help" in the process of healing by siphoning the life out of vulnerable individuals in order to skim off the excess for themselves.

With a grooming motion, Reb Yoel kept moving his paired palms inches above the putrefying flesh. Now it was time to invoke the aid of the Great Seven.

"In the name of Ya-weh, who created heaven and earth, and in the names of the seven archangels," he chanted repeatedly, "Michael, Gabriel, and Raphael, Aniel, Kaftziel, Tzadkiel, and Samael." Each time he called on these greatest of divine messengers to dispel the demons of disease, the roomful of villagers responded with a solemn "Amen."

Reb Yoel now saw the thinnest of flames streaming out from all of his fingers. They merged into a light-sleeve that enveloped the stricken leg. Their combined strength left much to be desired, however. One of the Great Ones had arrived...but clearly showed little enthusiasm, he thought.

Glancing out at the room, he saw someone walking freely among the study tables in direct defiance of Nazi orders to stay put. It was a heavy-set man in a shabby business suit. His dark, pock-marked features lay half hidden beneath a bushy gray beard. Yossl Mandelstam! Yossl was proprietor of that secondhand bookstore off Franz Josefs Kai in Vienna where Yoel had occasionally stumbled upon some rare old Kabbalistic text. So poor Yossl was permanently out of business! Yoel clucked his tongue. Never, to please a customer, had Yossl scurried among his dust-laden shelves as energetically as he dashed about here. He had already gathered a fistful of threads from the chests of most of the villagers. None of them paid him any more mind than the guards did.

It was thus that the Presences announced themselves—in the form of someone Yoel knew, someone no longer among the living. Yossl advanced now toward Yoel clutching a ball of silver threads stretching like kite-strings from the breastbones of the villagers.

"You'd better call for more help, Yoel," he said, dividing the bundle of strand-ends evenly before placing a clump in each of Yoel's hands. "Your townsmen don't seem to have much pep. Not that I blame these lantzmen of yours. Fear alone isn't enough to coax the best out of them. And on a diet of potatoes and beets, they can hardly keep their own flesh from stinking. And look at your Rabbi Dovidl. Nothing from him at all! I don't think he gets the picture," he said, twirling a finger significantly near his ear.

"What happened to you, Yossl?"

"They got me," he said, nodding over at the

fidgety colonel who sat on the bench in front of the stove. The soldiers who stood like bookends on either side of the bench were equally oblivious to Yossl. "I was in hiding till they caught me six months ago. I hand it to you, you lucky gonif, hustling your tukhis out of Vienna.... Anyway, Yoel, this is all I can squeeze out of this roomful of doddering old wind bags."

"I'll work with whatever you give me, Yossl."

"What a grave you've settled in, Yoel! There isn't even a book here I could sell in my shop. They're antiques, sure, but they're fingered to shreds, and the covers are hanging by a thread."

"All day the men sit and read here, Yossl."

"Ekh!" The bookseller threw up his hands in disgust. "I'll get out of your way. Just call on more Names—and don't let your mind wander, not for a second!"

"I know, Yossl. Good-bye, Yossl." Yoel continued to massage the air above the hopeless-looking leg. He now began to call on all the other angels he could think of, not a whit embarrassed at doing so, knowing he needed all the assistance he could muster.

"Come forth from the portals of heaven! Turn back the hours of the sick one! Come, Uriel, Hagalel, Tubuar, Inias. Descend and unravel the skein of his days! Come, Tibuel, Sabaoc, Simiel! We give you each a portion of our own precious hours so that taken all together, they may balance the ledgers of

Shaddai, who alone gives you the power to reverse the clock of affliction and restore this limb to health."

And repeatedly he called on additional angelic entities who he thought might lend a hand if they weren't occupied elsewhere, like Shamriel, Khasdiel, Khaniel, and Rachmiel; not to mention the famed troika who could fight off Lilith herself: "Come, Sanvi, Sansanvi, Semangelaf, and roll back the cataract of blight!"

The flickering finger-flames thickened and broadened. Soon, Yoel's hands poured rivers of fire into the luminescent sheath encircling the leg. The captain's limb began to undergo changes. Yoel took note of the flush of new blood at the fringes of the infection. The scarlet streaks of poison that climbed the threatened thigh began to pale, to begin their retreat, to play their history backward.

Everyone in the room sensed the change in Yoel's mood. There was a hush of expectancy. The old folks of Drozh strained forward, giving yet more of the little they could afford, providing the fuel that powered Yoel's mode of healing. The ceremony went on for two hours, Yoel confidently invoking ever more of the heavenly host: Zelioz, Ramathel, Morael, Pakhadron, and even the Tetragrammaton Himself. Whoever the attendant Presences were, gradually they wound the clock of sepsis backward.

The colonel leaned forward more often as changes made themselves evident. Yoel could feel that "Herr Oberst"'s skepticism was melting. Boredom and impatience began grudgingly to retire from his clean-shaven, smooth-skinned, hawkish, narrow-eyed face, a face that never lost an underlying hardness of expression.

At the retreating edges of the infection, up from the toes and down from the thigh, the color of the ravaged flesh progressively lightened. Grays, blacks, and purples blanched to greens, to reds, to pink. Puffy pockets of waterlogged skin crumpled, disappeared; withered patches, like fields of scorched earth, turned smoother, rounder, plumper. So impressed despite himself was the colonel—who had been exercising remarkable restraint—that he removed his officer's cap and held it to his chest as if out of awe and respect (unmindful, of course, that he was seated within the walls of a synagogue). Yoel thought that once or twice he had even heard the colonel whisper "Amen!"

By now the captain was fully conscious. With new-found energy bracing himself up on his elbows, he stared in silence at his utterly transformed leg. Finally, the colonel stood up over the captain. Stone-faced, he gazed at a perfectly normal-looking limb. Around the original wound there remained only a hint of soreness.

"How do you feel, Captain Von Steinhausen?"

The officer sprang to his feet and walked tentatively around over the blanket. "Amazing! I found myself dreaming back in time, day by day, right back to the day of my wound, and to the moment before I was wounded. I feel perfectly...sound, sir."

"Are you sure this is not merely some illusion, Sternberg?" asked the colonel.

"Illusion, sir?"

"A magician's trick?"

Suddenly there was a disturbance in the room. Like a drunkard, Rabbi Dovidl came stumbling forward toward the colonel. Froth edged his lips. His fists flailed the air.

"Stop!" shouted Sergeant Gerhardt.

"Rebbe!" said Yoel, reaching out to break his lunge.

"Out! Out of here, you murdering Schwein- hund! You and your devils from hell!" The rabbi's fist did not even reach the lapel it vaguely struck at. Sergeant Gerhardt charged forward and rammed the old man in the chin with the butt of his weapon. As he fell to the floor, he hit him again—in the head. Blood poured simultaneously from the rabbi's mouth and forehead. People screamed and rushed forward. The guards, swinging machine-guns around, barked at everyone to stay put. Yoel, kneeling down next to him, saw that the rebbe had ceased breathing. He focused all his remaining energies, tented his hands above the old man's head, broke into a mumbled in- cantation ....

"Up, Sternberg!" said the colonel. Sergeant Gerhardt jerked him backward and up off his knees.

"Old age makes people a little feebleminded, doesn't it, Sternberg?" said the colonel. "But because of your exemplary services, I shall exact no further retribution for his stupid attack. Get your coat on and come with us. I have further work for you to do back at my unit."

"Forgive me, Herr Oberst," said Yoel, daring to object. "But I thought we made a bargain, like gentlemen."

"We did. And we are leaving your village in peace. As to you, we will release you as soon as we have no further need for you."

Sergeant Gerhardt shoved him from behind, and Reb Yoel bit his tongue. He felt that he personally was doomed, but for now his only wish was that the Germans would take him away without killing any more of the others.

"The salt! Don't forget your salt!" said the colonel, thrusting the tin shaker into Reb Yoel's hand.

Colonel Knatte was pleased to see that the two men left outside had done a fine job removing the morning's dew from his jeep. The olive hood gleamed again under the pale midday sun. The few dents it bore were barely visible amidst the sheen.

Barely visible, that is, to the untrained eye—but the colonel knew every pit and scratch that marred the glimmering skin, knew what the polishing tried to hide.

At first he thought he would throw the Jew among his half-dozen infantrymen in the back of the truck. But as much as Sternberg gave him the shivers, he felt that having him ride with him was like wearing a lucky charm. He had him sit in the back with the reanimated Von Steinhausen. The blanket that protected the seat-cushions was big enough to fit under both of them.

The truck bounced on over the winding, rutted road about fifty meters ahead of the colonel's jeep. Patches of evergreens, now sparse, now thick, spread open on either side of them like spiked jaws gaping before an oncoming swallow. But Russia had just swallowed them! thought Knatte. And now she was spitting them out, running in reverse the reel spun out by the master projectionist in Berlin.

"Sternberg," said the colonel, who was relieved to be out in the cold, crisp air, far from the stink of the little synagogue, "I found your performance uncanny.... Keep well bundled up, captain, until we find you a new pair of pants—and your other boot as well."

"When a man combines the skills of a Jewish physician and a country healer, sir, maybe it is not all that uncanny after all," said the captain.

"Perhaps, Sternberg, you can make this giant blister called Russia disappear too?" The colonel felt his spirits reviving. He was glad for the renewed sparkle of his jeep, in some way even gladder than for the rosy glow of the captain's renewed leg. The jeep seemed far more dependable than the captain. After all, even with General Von Steinhausen's influence, would the High Command excuse Colonel Knarre for the annihilation of his brigade—not to mention his getting lost during the retreat? Hitler would be unsparing in casting blame. Disgrace seemed more likely than "promotion," he thought, whatever the captain's condition when they finally reached Minsk!

But what if the Russians got there first? he wondered. What if they were all heading into a trap? Maybe he ought to forget about Minsk, head south toward Hungary...and from there try to make it across Austria. Then, perhaps, via Italy, into the safety of Switzerland! "I asked you a question, Sternberg. Can you make Russia disappear?"

"It would be presumptuous of me to compare myself, Herr Oberst, to all the armed might of Germany."

He should have killed Mr. Magician on the spot for that remark; instead, he found himself laughing uncontrollably. The captain quickly joined in the laughter, while Sergeant Gerhardt drove on unsmiling.

"We should present Mr. Sternberg to Hitler as

147

a new secret weapon," said the colonel.

"Or as a cure for insanity," added the captain. Sergeant Gerhardt, in a moment of failed attention, did something to grind the gears.

"I would be cautious about such jokes, Captain, no matter who your father is!" said the colonel. Not only did the conversation come to a halt, but the jeep soon rolled to a stop as well, in spite of Gerhardt's hundred Verdammtes and frantic fiddling with gearshift, gas pedal and choke.

"Start it up again, Gerhardt!"

"I'm trying, sir." A weak mutter came from the engine. Feebler responses followed.

"Are we out of gas, sergeant?"

"Not if this gauge is correct, sir."

"Did your stupid driving a moment ago flood the engine, sergeant?"

"The engine does not appear to be flooded, sir."

"Well, why do you sit there like an idiot? Go out and check under the hood!"

"Yes, sir."

The truck up ahead stopped and ground backward. Now that the colonel was motionless himself, he could observe the shivering motions of the forest, from the monumental swaying of the treetops down to the skittering of small creatures against a backdrop of perfect camouflage. The birds that darted overhead looked like bats, vultures, pterodactyls, not like any crows he knew in Germany. What else might be hiding among the shifting shadows? he wondered. A rifle barrel? A partisan signaling to his cronies? "Well, what is it, Gerhardt?"

"I think it may be the battery, sir." Two men jumped out of the back of the truck and ran up to the colonel's jeep.

"Careful with your filthy hands!" said the colonel. He poked his head out from under the canvas flap and glared at them. "Can't you see it's just been waxed?"

"Jawohl!" The men seemed to know what they were doing. They tinkered with this and that. They came to the same conclusion as Sergeant Gerhardt. "Give us your cables and we'll give you a jump-start," one of them said to Gerhardt.

"We don't have any cables," said Gerhardt, slamming the hood closed—to Knatte's further irritation.

"You absolute idiot! We came out here and you did not think of bringing along cables?" With every wasted second the colonel felt a nameless, faceless terror pressing in from every side. That Russian peasant had deliberately set them up for an ambush! He'd been working in collusion with the Jew!

"There are no cables left in what's left of the entire squadron, sir!" said Gerhardt, throwing his hands like penguin flippers out to his bulky sides.

The hair on the colonel's neck bristled as he thought of the Jew sitting behind him. The Jew, who commanded strange powers as a healer, was in some way responsible for the power-loss unaccountably incurred by their battery. "What do you suggest we do, then?" asked the colonel. He looked all around him.

"We have no choice but to abandon the jeep and go back in the truck," said the captain.

"How dare you suggest that I abandon this jeep, Captain?" The colonel shivered with rage. "Did I abandon you even though you were already among the dead as far as anyone with common sense could see?"

"Herr Oberst, forgive me, I did not mean to ...."

Everyone fell into such deep silence that the colonel could hear the cawing of birds that might just be the sorts of signals employed by partisans grouping in the woods. What's happening to me? he wondered. He was falling victim to his imagination. In another second he'd be cowering beneath his jeep if he didn't get hold of himself. In this part of Russia there were no partisans in the woods, just trenchfuls of lead-filled Jews. It was a miracle that the only Jew of any real use had eluded the SS dragnet! He took a deep breath and determined to stay calm. Crows were crows, cawing was cawing, and that was all there was to it.

"Might I make a suggestion, sir?"

The colonel looked around at Sternberg in surprise.

"Speak up, Sternberg!"

"That the jeep be towed back. Surely there is a rope, a sturdy rope?"

The colonel was incensed. It was an obvious idea. Of course they carried rope. But not a single German had yet thought to mention it! He would make this Jew pay for being presumptuous. "Sternberg, forget the rope. We are driving back, proudly, in this very jeep, and you are going to repair it! And if you don't, Sternberg, I shall use our rope for your neck."

"Me, sir? Repair your jeep?"

"Get out, Sternberg! Wave your hands over the hood where the battery is and bring the jeep back to life." The soldiers laughed. The embarrassing tension was broken. The colonel had no thought of dispensing so quickly with the services of this Viennese "expatriate." His troops, after witnessing the captain's recovery, expected the Jew's talents to be applied to the wounded of lesser rank back at camp. The colonel needed to restore morale, to undercut the vicious rumors, relayed to him by his driver, that their Kommandant had gotten them all hopelessly lost. When they did finally hook up with a medically functioning unit, then the healer would be quietly gotten rid of. There would be no official mention, requiring awkward explanations, that the colonel had resorted to "racially impure" means to reduce the casualty rate among his troops. "The salt, Sternberg! Don't forget your salt!"

Reb Yoel climbed out as commanded. He walked around to the front of the jeep and pictured his whole situation: grinning soldiers, frowning colonel, and a bored-looking captain who could not afford to say thank-you to a subhuman. "This is a job for demons," warned Yoel, knowing how absurd he must sound. "Demons should not be called upon except in direst emergencies." He remembered the peasants losing their crops, the urgency of their pleas, the reluctance he felt even then to intervene for a good cause. "It is only fair to tell you in advance, sir, that demons are extortionate in the payment they exact for their services."

The driver and the other two soldiers broke out into laughter.

"Ah-hah!" said the colonel. "So the demons are Jews too! Well, Sternberg, since they are friends of yours, you should be able to get our jeep running at cut-rate prices, shouldn't you?" The soldiers guffawed without restraint, slapping their knees and pounding each other's chests.

Reb Yoel politely joined in the laughter. He hoped, however, that the joke would now be over and that the colonel was merely punishing him for offering unbidden advice. But the colonel was dead serious. "What are you waiting for, Sternberg?" he snapped.

Reb Yoel stared at the mildly dented hood. "I will need the cooperation of everyone I can get. The other soldiers, too. The more to supply the energy, the less the cost to each—I hope."

"You will get the cooperation you require," said the colonel. He ordered the remaining troops out of the truck, ignoring a muffled remark from the captain. "But don't take too long, you hear?" He looked at his watch. I'll give you...exactly ten minutes."

Reb Yoel steeled himself, refusing to show fear.

"We are losing valuable time," muttered the captain.

"I give the orders here, Captain," said the colonel.

Reb Yoel stressed the need for everyone to concentrate, to visualize energy pouring back into the battery, and not to mind his strange incantations. He prepared himself by praying in Hebrew for God's forgiveness for the sin he was about to commit, the sin of invoking the myrmidons of Satan to effect change in the realm over which he presided, the realm of the dead, the world of inanimate matter, the *tohu vavohu*. And then Yoel called upon some of the minor mazzikim, Dagon and Belial, pagan fiends subdued by the ancient Israelites.

He made a show of casting salt over the hood, but in this ceremony salt was uncalled for, since now the presence of most demons was invited. His palms moved out in slow, counter-rotating circles, like miniature swimming strokes, inches above the section of the hood that overlay the battery.

As he uttered the demons' names, he felt a searing sensation in his hands, as if the steam from an overheated radiator had sprayed them. At the same time his ears rang with thousands of voices from the forest. They demanded him to stop, but he was in no position to pay heed to them.

Blasts of wind whipped through the trees and tore at the soldiers' coats. A pair of crows, their sun-flecked feathers shining gun-metal blue, swooped down from the branches above. They made passes over the jeep, swiped at the startled faces of the troops, flitted in circles like disoriented bats. Their flight-paths followed the pattern that was traced by Reb Yoel's hands, from which a reddish glow descended onto the hood of the jeep.

The Germans bent forward and followed Reb Yoel's hands as if mesmerized. He imagined tubes strapped to their necks through which streams of their blood were trickling through the tips of his fingers. He noted the strain on his captors, the creases forming in their brows.

"Shouldn't we be getting out of here?" said the captain, puncturing the solemn silence, tearing the invisible tube from his neck.

The colonel glanced at his watch, relieved at the captain's intervention. "Enough nonsense!" he said, turning the key in the ignition. Before the troops could laugh, the engine kicked over.

Only Sergeant Gerhardt laughed. "That often happens, Herr Oberst," he said. "You think the battery's dead, you let it rest a while, and then poof! It's got just enough juice again to—"

"Shut up, sergeant! I don't want to hear your stupidly obvious explanations. Get in and let's get moving. The demons do not have large appetites today, do they, Sternberg?"

Reb Yoel lifted the side-flap, climbed back in beside the captain, and held his tongue.

The truck kept 50 meters ahead, and the journey proceeded in silence—except for the cracking and booming sounds that echoed from far in front of them. They were not the sounds of thunder, lightning, or wind. For a while no one commented, but the noises persisted.

"It's the Russians," said the captain. "I hear planes."

"I think you are right," said the colonel.

"How far away could they be?"

"Not far."

"Who do you think they're attacking?" asked the captain.

"Us," said the colonel. "Our camp.... Keep driving, Gerhardt, you fool!" The drone of aircraft grew louder as the jeep rolled over the brow of a hill that was sparsely covered with trees. The sun, still high in the sky, seemed to Reb Yoel like a spotlight trained on them alone, relentlessly tracking their little procession, whose advance seemed suddenly pointless.

"What do you think we should do, sir?" said the captain.

"Return to our unit."

"They must be taking quite a beating."

"I agree, captain."

"There may be nothing left of our unit, sir. Listen, sir!" A pair of planes hummed by them high overhead. "I think we should take cover, sir."

"I'm sure they haven't seen us, captain."

The truck speeded up and Gerhardt followed suit. The woods offered better cover a few hundred meters ahead. But an ear-splitting roar shook the frozen earth beneath them as the low-flying planes returned. The colonel seemed taken by surprise. He shouted something to the driver, but Gerhardt ceased driving just as the heavens exploded with machine-gun fire and bombs burst directly in front of them. The vehicle ahead of them vanished in flame and thunder.

Reb Yoel dropped to the floor, deafened by the crack of bullets, blinded by the dust and burning debris that rained upon the jeep from the luckless truck in the lead. The motion of the jeep was erratic. Yoel scrambled up to see what was happening.

With his left hand the colonel had gripped the wheel over the slouching body of Gerhardt, directing the jeep in among the meager clumps of pines beside the road.

The canvas flap beside the driver was torn to shreds. Gerhardt groaned. He called for the colonel. The colonel's right hand appeared, pointing a pistol at Gerhardt's head—unsteadily, given the jouncing of the vehicle. With a single shot, and a simultaneous push, the colonel rolled Sergeant Gerhardt out onto the ground.

The jeep bounced further into the scraggly woods, and the captain now decided to commandeer the whole back seat. He hurled himself at Reb Yoel, who had no room to get out of his way. Reb Yoel turned to look him in the face but could focus only on the blood that bubbled freely from his shattered right temple.

"Von Steinhausen!" shouted the colonel after bringing the jeep to a halt.

"The captain is wounded, Herr Oberst."

The colonel turned and stared. He raised his weapon, almost contemplatively, then thrust it in Reb Yoel's face. "Throw him out, Sternberg. Keep his brains on the blanket. I don't want him messing up any more of the back seat."

"Yes, Herr Oberst." There was blood on every part of the captain. Reb Yoel fought against vomiting as he dragged the officer out and laid him next to a tree.

The colonel got out and looked up at the sky. "They are not returning," he said flatly. "Look at the mess they've made of this jeep. Just look!" Cinders; fragments of wood, glass and metal; frozen clods of earth and pine-needles spattered every surface of the vehicle. On the driver's side, the grille and windshield were shattered, the hood was mangled, and the canvas top in tatters. The colonel ran a black-gloved hand over the wounds in the buckled hood. "See, Sternberg? Bullet holes straight along the entire right side. They got Gerhardt and the captain in a single strafing run. And look at the bloody mess in the driver's seat!" He took off his cap, flicked the dust off, then carefully set it back on his head.

Reb Yoel now felt certain that the colonel intended to shoot him. He glanced all around for a course to run that put trees between himself and the Luger.

"You don't think they'll let me into Switzerland in a jeep looking like this, do you, Sternberg?"

"I don't know, sir."

"Of course not. But I'm not at all worried. Do you know why?"

"No, sir."

"Because you are going to repair it."

"Me?... Perhaps with some tools, sir—"

"Forget the tools! First, a little housecleaning. There are rags under the driver's seat. Wipe the muck off this vehicle. Quick!" Reb Yoel did as he was told. "I watched what you did when you worked on the battery, Sternberg."

"I can't take credit for that, sir."

"Don't lie to me! There was a dent in the hood right above the battery. It was completely smoothed out during the course of your little seance."

"I don't remember such a dent, sir, but —"

"Call upon all the devils in hell if you have to, Sternberg! But make this jeep like new, do you hear? And when you're through, I'll let you go free. You have the word of an officer and a gentleman!" said the colonel, waving his weapon across his chest in a flourish.

"But there's only the two of us, colonel."

"So what?"

"Even if I could summon up certain forces, which is by no means to be taken for granted, sir, they can do nothing more than channel the energies of the living, and if they were to see such a limited supply...." Reb Yoel shuddered to think of what might happen. The demons were an unpredictable lot. They could ignore the summons altogether, or, if treated with ritual carelessness, they could turn their insatiable thirst against their conjurer. Had that singeing heat in his hands been a warning of sorts? Only when no other alternative presented itself did Reb Yoel ever call upon the demons.

Knatte had begun to look darkly at him from below the rim of his cap. "Your salt is in your pocket,

Sternberg!"

"All right, Herr Oberst," said Yoel, spraying salt over the vehicle in a complicated, meaningless pattern.  "As you say, 'all the devils in hell,' sir." He was resolved to try as he had never before in his life.

"You are sounding more confident.  Good!"

Reb Yoel cast down the filthy rags he'd been using.  "Please stand here, near the hood, sir.  And fix in mind, if you will, an image of how this vehicle must have looked brand-new."  He himself stood in front of the jeep.  Extending his arms over the hood, he petitioned heaven's protection for what he was about to attempt.  He trembled with apprehension, for he would now dare call upon the king of demons, Ashmedai himself!  And not only him, but his queen, Igrat, and Makhlat mother of Igrat too!  He summoned them each, seven times.

Hardly had he ended his third invocation when numberless voices assaulted his ears once more. They harangued him, they implored him, filling his mind with their tears.  Filtered through the forest floor, bubbling up through earth-choked mouths, pleading from the vastness of their collective graves, they begged Reb Yoel to stop, to give no aid and comfort to their, and his own, mortal enemy.  Long they persisted, wringing his heart, warning against the demons, gnawing at his concentration.  Heavy with their grief, Reb Yoel paid them homage in the only way he could—by refusing to accede to their demands.    At last, a rising wind drowned out the wailing voices.  Howling over the scrubby plateau, it stung Reb Yoel's hands till the tips of his fingers turned blue.

These were the "scout" winds, the advance guard, he knew, a nameless band of ruahim ra'im, or evil spirits, sent out to test the mettle of the invoker. Soon a flock of sparrows wheeled high up over the jeep, swooped as if to attack, then  rapidly soared away.  Always they kept their distance, probing for a weak spot, a point of entry into the soul.  These were the indiscriminate angels of destruction, the malak kabbal, that took without giving.  They gathered opportunistically at every conjuration.  And with every sixth breath, Reb Yoel uttered the six-worded Shema  in the hope of fending them off.

As the winds died down, an unseasonable swarm of horseflies gathered above the jeep.  They landed on the colonel's shoulders and he flailed at them with his cap.  "Why  don't they bother you?" snarled the colonel.  But these, Yoel knew, were the legions of Beelzebub, Lord of the Flies and Grand Lieutenant of Ashmedai.  They were a surly lot that he had to keep addressing in the name of their overlord if he was to hold them strictly to task.

Suddenly the flies were gone, vanishing as rapidly as they had come.  And moments later Reb Yoel saw beside him the hunched-over form of Rabbi Dovidl.

"You're a troublemaker, Yoel! If it weren't for you I'd be perfectly all right." The rabbi shook his finger at Yoel.

"I apologize, Reb Dovidl."

"I thought I hired you to do the odd jobs, Yoel. And now you want my help? And all you give me to work with is one fehshtunkene Nazi? And this one, no less? Oy Gott!" The rabbi made a twirling motion with his finger near his ear.

Colonel Knatte stared at the jeep and the Jew, Jew and jeep, jeep and Jew. He refused to allow his eyes to play tricks on him. Did things keep flickering in the uneven polish of the metal? Birds. Just birds! he thought. In a moment of glaring lucidity he understood that his rational faculties were in the grip of wishful thinking! Had he expected this lousy jeep of his to last for a thousand years? Could it bolster his punctured dignity? Save him from the cesspool of history? It was a scrap-heap, and he along with it, and Gerhardt, and Von Steinhausen too!

He felt angry with himself. Sternberg was tricking him just to gain time, hoping that the planes would return, hoping that luck would strike again in his favor. But in all fairness, as an officer and a gentleman, he would have to give the Jew a

*These were the indiscriminate angels of destruction....*

chance to prove himself. Having deceived himself thus far, the colonel had nothing to lose by waiting another few minutes—and everything to lose if he listened to his own common sense! Strange paradox indeed! It made him tired to think. His ears still buzzed from the bombing—or was it the hum of those winged maggots roused by the smell of blood from their sleep?

"Herr Oberst, Herr Oberst!"

Startled, the colonel glanced to his right to see the limping form of his chauffeur only twenty meters away. "Gerhardt! I thought you were...."

"Did you really expect me to abandon you, now that you need me the most, my colonel?" Gerhardt came up beside him. A wound showed clearly above his right ear and his chest was drenched in blood. Without any further ado, the sergeant whipped a clean rag out of the colonel's own coat sleeve. Knatte did not remember having put it there.

"You are still bleeding, Gerhardt!"

"The fate of grunts like me is to bleed, sir. We bleed so that leaders like you may safeguard the honor of Germany. Just look at the mess I made in my seat, sir. But don't you worry." In no time at all, Gerhardt wiped away all the bloodstains! "This jeep'll look like new in a jiffy. Have I ever let you down before, sir?"

"Of course not, Gerhardt, but—"

Ignoring the mumbling Jew, the colonel watched Gerhardt rub away at the blasted hood—and even sweep his cloth over the riddled canvas. The sergeant scrubbed with a miserable rag that seemed to focus the rays of the sun and glow ever more brightly as he worked. But what was the point of that ridiculous polishing? The logic completely escaped him. Gerhardt was out of his mind! thought Knatte. And as to that rag the sergeant was using—whenever the colonel looked directly at the rag, the end seemed still to be emerging from his sleeve, like a magician's endless scarf! But when he looked back at his sleeve, the mirage disappeared, of course; and he put it all down to hallucinations.

"I do admire your cunning, sir," Gerhardt chuckled.

"What cunning, Gerhardt?"

"In your shiny new jeep you should have no trouble making it to Switzerland."

"How dare you, sergeant!" Knatte was stunned. "Do you know that I could have you shot for such a remark?" How could Gerhardt know? Had he let drop a playful remark to the captain within earshot of his driver? But now the colonel began to be distracted by undeniable changes. They were occurring right under his nose. Puckering bullet holes slowly closed up—like the dents made by fingers in dough. The frozen snarl of twisted grillwork was stretching out, curling back to its vertical position. Tears in the green cloth were knitting themselves together. Either the sun was playing tricks on him, or Gerhardt was, or the Jew....

"After all, you have every right to look after yourself now, Colonel. You are a rotten failure, yes, but look at your superiors!" said Gerhardt, still wiping.

"You are speaking treason and accusing me of...the same," choked the colonel, his voice weak, a great weight pressing on his chest. The reviving jeep revived memories of before-the-war, when he managed one of the biggest paint factories in Germany. He thought fleetingly of his wife, and of his two boys who were fighting on another front. But each time he recalled something personally important, it receded into a dim, distant past. He could not stop the outflow of memories, draining like blood from his brain—but did they really matter anyway? he wondered. Knatte began to shiver from top to bottom. The wind sliced through his sleeves. His coat was too big! He wrapped it closer around him, hugging protruding bones.

"Oh yes, I envy you the fancy life in Switzerland. Or is it to America you are heading with this jeep, sir?"

"Silence!"

"But you will never get to either place, my colonel."

"I will get to Switzerland, Gerhardt, you swine-faced Swabian filth! If only my hand had been steadier!"

"You are down to about twelve liters of fuel, Herr Oberst. Your supplies are now destroyed along

167

with your unit.  At best you'd have wound up in a stalled jeep on a barren steppe, alone in the frozen heart of Russia."

"Enough!"  A garbled croak came out of the colonel's dust-dry mouth.  He raised his weapon at the chattering chauffeur, but it fell from a wrist gone limp.  He stooped to retrieve it, but his legs collapsed and he wound up supporting himself with his elbows on the hood of the jeep.

"Look at the finish, sir!  The finish!" said Gerhardt, pointing at the colonel's reflection.

Colonel Knatte stared into the mirror-like hood and another man stared back.  The stiff officer's cap, far too large for the head, flopped over a face whose features were those of a stranger.  Shrunken and wrinkled, they bore some resemblance to his grandfather's, perhaps, but certainly not to....

He shook his head as if to say no, and the absurd cap fell off a bald, gray dome about as big as the knob of the synagogue door in Drozh.  Only a few white wisps fringed the ridiculously large ears or else stuck like little brushes out of the nostrils. The colonel scraped at the hood of the beautiful jeep, but his hands slid out of his oversized gloves. The gnarled fingers, helplessly slipping, clawed desperately at the factory-polished metal.

Reb Yoel repeated the Shema seven times, and seven times the prayer for the departure of all evil spirits. He was exhausted. He felt as if days had gone by, but the position of the sun told him that little more than two hours had passed. He had managed to beat off the worst of the attacks; he had made hardly a slip. The frustrated demons were furious, insatiable. They had fed, but not enough, and now he had forced them to disperse. Nor did the voices from beneath the snow return to assail him anymore.

A cold wind whistled through the mangy wood. Reb Yoel looked down at the shriveled remains of the ancient Colonel Knatte. He pocketed only his service pistol—to turn over some day to the partisans. And there was, of course, no sin attached to the confiscation of abandoned vehicles. How else was he supposed to get home?

He looked the jeep over carefully. The demons had missed a little spot here and there that could still use touching up. Perhaps if they'd had just a little more time—but the colonel had given them all the time he had left.

Reb Yoel sat in the driver's seat. He turned the key and the engine hummed. Even the glass of the windshield looked brand new.

# The Night of the Leavened Bread

by Mark Blackman

MARK BLACKMAN has sent his interplanetary creation, Baruch Rogers, Space Rabbi, hurtling through space on a number of occasions, most recently in the radio play *The Wrath of Cohen*. If you missed that performance, here's a chance to meet the Rabbi as he performs one of his most daring, and ennobling feats of kashrut.

This story is based on the Passover eve adage: The bigger they rise, the harder they fall.

*S*omething's not kosher in your neighborhood? Who're ya gonna call?

"Enter freely and of your own will. And wipe
your feet off." Lightning crackled across the sky
and by its light and the silvery moons', Baruch
Rogers, Space Rabbi huddled in the doorway of the
castle. From across the Translevoneh hills came a
mournful howling. "Wolves," said the bent figure.
"Children of the night."

"Well, the Wolfs might teach their children a little consideration. People could be trying to sleep."
The doorway opened fully and Rogers stepped inside. He regarded the man who had let him in. His
twisted torso made it difficult for the Rabbi to judge
his size. One arm jutted out and an unkempt white
mane made him seem likelier to be some sort of riff-
raff than the baleboss, or master of the house. "Good
evening. I am Baruch Rogers, Space Rabbi. I'm
here about preparations for *yontif,* Pesach to be exact.
Are you 2 4 995 + tax?"

"No, I'm just the help. My name is Yizkor."

173

He nodded in greeting; his body remained in a hunched-over position. "I'll take you to him. Walk this way."

Yizkor strode forward, his right shoulder stuck out wide, head far up and back, and left shoulder tilted. One leg shuffled slowly across the floor. Rogers swiftly cut off YENTA's audio circuit before his the ship's computer could retrieve the appropriate punchline.

It had been years since the Rabbi had visited the white castle. At the time it was being converted from a hamburger (and frankfurter) restaurant to a bakery. Rogers had re-koshered the establishment. Since then, the bakery had gotten a new proprietor and a new name, and even the address had been changed to 221B Bakery Street, after the current enterprise. Tonight the Rabbi was here to help the baker rid his shop and home of all *chometz*, or leavened products, in preparation for Pesach.

When humankind headed out to the stars, it brought with it not only its technology but its civilization and laws as well. While police were needed to enforce the civil laws, it was left to others to preserve the religious lore. Judaism, as a religion governed by time-honored rites and customs, took great pains to adapt to the new technological environment. In the face of modern technology, rabbis had long had to interpret the Law and make new rulings. With stellar diaspora, that role not only continued, but expanded. As the

Space Age progressed, so too did the Rabbinate.

Baruch Rogers, Space Rabbi voyaged from planet to planet in his interstellar *mitzvahmobile*, asking colonists, "Are you Jewish? Did you put on *tefillin* this morning?" and passing on the kashrut, or kosherness, of alien life-forms. Once, the Rebbe encountered an offog, the *Moishe Kapoyra* of the exoanimal kingdom. Like the famous Yiddish cartoon character, it did things backwards; instead of having cloven hooves and chewing its cud, it had a cloven cud and chewed its hooves. He had just declared the alien mammalian *trefe* and the creature, insulted, attacked him, not caring that the Rabbi himself was nonkosher. It did not take the great scholar long to realize that since the creature was *trefe* he did not need a *shochet* to slaughter it. Fortunately, after a moment's initial rage, the beast realized this as well. It later joined the Rebbe for the Shabbat meal, though it kept strictly vegetarian.

Rogers was led past cases displaying various breads, *mandel broit*, and *hamantashen* left over from Purim. "Excuse me but I couldn't help noticing that you seem to have a small problem." The Rabbi spoke slowly and carefully. "Have you considered seeing a doctor?"

"A doctor?" the little man exclaimed. "What for do I want a doctor? A tailor I need. Look at this suit - this sleeve is two inches too long, the collar is halfway up my head, and the left shoulder is two inches wider than the right! And you wouldn't believe how the pants pull in the back!" He led Baruch through a narrow doorway. "Here we are, Rabbi. Welcome to the Little Shop of Challahs."

A heavyset man in a white apron scurried from oven to oven. In the center of the room stood the second-largest oven tray the Rabbi had ever seen. Something massive lay covered under a sheet of waxed paper. Rogers audibly cleared his throat.

The baker looked up. "Oh, you must be the Rabbi. I'm Raphael 2 4 995 + tax."

"How do you do, Mr. Plus Tax. That's funny, you don't look Jewish. I see you've already gathered together the chometz. There's still some left in the front of your shop though."

"Call me Raphael. 2 4 995 + tax isn't my real name. It used to be Loew; I changed it for business reasons. And this isn't just chometz." His eyes gleamed. "It's my masterpiece. I, Rabbi, am going to create life! Under that sheet lies a Golem."

Dramatic music swelled up around them. "Oops, sorry," said Yizkor. "I turned on the radio to get the latest soccer scores."

"A Golem?" Rogers was stunned. "The very idea is half-baked."

"Nu, so's the Golem. It's an old family recipe handed down for generations, going back to the time of the Maharal."

The Rebbe gasped. Of course, he realized. Loew, as in Rabbi Yehuda Loew of Prague. Hundreds of years ago on Earth, using the power of

*HaShem*, the Divine Name, he had brought a clay effigy to pseudo life to protect the Jews of the ghetto. Could this baker....

"It's been a dream I've carried since before I had the pretzel stand outside Jerusalem's lot. Of course, I've modified the recipe a little. Instead of clay I used dough mixed with swamp things. A *bissel Kabbalah*, a *bissel* Sara Lee. And I adapted it for the microwave." He yanked off the waxed paper and slid the tray into the oven before it.

"Well, now we know what he did last *Shevat*." The voice of the Space Rabbi's ship's computer sounded quietly in his helmet's earpiece. So much for cutting off his audio link. The Yiddiskeit-programmed Ethnocentric Nomothetic Talmudic Analytic computer Series 18, YENTA for short, did more than astrogate his vessel, the JSS (Jewish-Starship) Mitzvah. Because of the hazards of spaceflight, rather than risk a set of sacred scrolls, YENTA had been programmed with the Torah and other books of Scripture, and the Talmud, the heart and soul of the Jewish people. He had also been programmed, thanks to the mysteriously long-lived Lazar Klein, the Senior Citizen of the Galaxy, with every Borscht Belt comedy routine ever written. This eclectic combination of programming had had some unusual consequences. There was, for instance, the time that YENTA had refused to open the pod bay doors for him and had subsequently serenaded the Rabbi with several choruses of "*Chad*

*Gad Yaw.*"  He had also gotten the *meshugge* idea that he was Jewish.

"A machine can't be a Jew!" the Rebbe had authoritatively pronounced, diplomatically ignoring the *yarmulka* sitting on the computer's central processing unit.  He was far more concerned about YENTA's *tzitzit* getting caught in his astrogation circuits.

YENTA's blue and white lights dimmed for a moment.  "Well, my mother was a CD-ROM of the Encyclopedia Judaica."

Rogers sighed.  "But a computer doesn't have a *ruach*, a soul, breath."

Unfazed, YENTA began emitting sounds that resembled an asthmatic breathing through the cowcatcher of an ancient steam locomotive, or, come to think of it, Dorf Feder, the Dark Landlord, inhaling and exhaling through his helmet's built-in respirator.  YENTA's next words staggered the Rabbi.  "Rebbe, I want to have a *brit*."

"But—but, we've never even established if you're, well, I mean, what gender, um, if you have, er....  And wouldn't you short out in a *mikvah*, the ritual bath?  What provision is there in *Halacha*, our code of law, for circumcising a computer?"

YENTA blinked.  Programmed with the thousands of years of wisdom of the great sages, it took but a nanosecond for him to extrapolate a response.  "A *mohel* can slice the shielding on a wire in my main data reproduction circuits.  And before you know it,

I'll be having a Bar Mitzvah. No timepieces as presents, though; I already have a chronometer built in."

Baruch Rogers felt just as unnerved now as he stood before Raphael's oven. "No, you mustn't," roared the Space Rabbi. "It's an *averah*, sacrilege!"

"Wild dogs couldn't make me change my mind." The oven began shining. "I'm sorry, Rabbi. Yes, what is it, Yizkor?"

His helper had reappeared at the doorway. "A busy evening this is, boss. There's a man from the Environmental Protection Agency who wants to know what you've been doing to the swamp. Right behind him is an inspector from the Health Department. And the meter reader."

The lights dimmed briefly as the oven drew more and more power. Lightning flashed across the sky, its flickers illuminating the momentary darkness.

"Tell them I'm not in. I can't be interrupted now at the culmination of my culinary triumph."

Yizkor turned (no easy feat in his ill-fitting suit) and left. A hush fell over the room, broken only by a clap of thunder and a soft ding.

Raphael opened the oven door and slid out the tray. "I hope it's not soup yet. No, it's hardening even as I watch." He reached into his apron pocket and extracted a piece of parchment. He affixed it to the Golem's rapidly drying forehead. "It's rising!"

"Sure it's not just the yeast?" Yizkor had

rejoined them.

The creature sat up. "It's alive! I've done it! I've created life!" trumpeted the baker.

"And I helped," Yizkor chimed in.

Rogers gasped. On the creature's forehead was the sacred Tetragrammaton.

"You see, Rabbi? I did everything by the Book." He turned to the creature. "Can you hear me? I created you. You must obey me. Do you understand?"

As if in response, there came an indistinct rumbling from the creature's throat. It swung around and lowered its feet to the floor. It stood, swaying for a moment, then began to lurch toward Raphael. The lumbering motion was far more graceful than Yizkor's. The Golem halted before the baker. And spoke. "*Vos - tut - zich*? What - is - going - on?"

It was Raphael's turn to be stunned. "He talks! Golems don't usually do that! They'll give me the Weizmann Institute Award for this! A chair at the Israel Institute of Technology! First Prize at my block party bake-off! I'll tell you what's going on," he said to the huge figure. "You're a Golem. I created you. You must —"

"No!" The Golem grabbed Raphael and swatted him aside. "*Ich darf*—I want—" It looked from the Rabbi to Yizkor. "Are you the... keymaster... the gatekeeper?

"Back off, I'm a Rabbi." The creature reached out to him. It slowly ran a hand down the front of

Baruch's black spacesuit, leaving small, wet clumps in his wake. "I've been *shmutzed*!" he groaned.

Yizkor turned to the Rabbi and shrugged. He faced the Golem. The creature bent down and mumbled into his ear. The Rabbi could not hear the question. "Second door on your left," stammered Yizkor.

*But the Golem never returned.*

"There goes the neighborhood," said Raphael. He was still nursing some minor bruises. "Every last person in the neighborhood is out here looking for my Golem, armed with torches. The whole city's in flight."

"Are you surprised?" asked Baruch Rogers. "After that rampage of his? Smashing gates, turning over groundcars, cutting in line at the deli counter?"

"And worst of all, he's never picked up a phone to call."

"Yes he has, boss," corrected Yitzkor. "He lifted up that booth at the corner of 13th Avenue and Mockingbird Lane."

"I tried to warn you, Raphael. You should never try to create a Golem except under strict rabbinical supervision. And speaking of phone calls, an acquaintance of mine, Fleisch Gordon, Attorney-at-Space-Law called. He represents the Block Association."

Two of the neighborhood residents halted near them.  One was wearing a hockey mask and carrying a hatchet.  The other wore a cowboy hat and was toting a chainsaw.  "*Shmattakopf*," said the first, "when we ordered torches we meant the kind with fire.  How are we supposed to burn that monster with flashlights?"

"You should have been more specific," said his companion.  "Besides, where do you expect me to find a firestarter in this rain?  The storm of the century it is out here."

"It's a regular nightmare on Elm Street.  Look, the monster's on Maple Street!"

"Good, I'm heading over to Addams!"

Yizkor joined his boss and the Rabbi.  "I had these signs made up," he said.  He waved a bunch of identical sheets of paper at them.  On each was an artist's rendering of the Golem and the words "WANTED BREAD OR ALIVE.  REWARD."  With each passing second, the downpour rendered them soggier.  "Excuse me," he said to them, then strode over to a man standing away from the mob, alone.  "Nachman, is that you?"

Nachman Beitz nodded to Yizkor, but declined the proffered handbill.  "I'm soaked to the skin," he said.  "I'm going home to take a shower."

"Rabbi, I'm worried about Yizkor."  It was Rogers' Yiddishkeit-programmed Ethnocentric Nomothetic Talmudic Analytic computer.  Minutes earlier, the baker's assistant had disappeared into the throng.

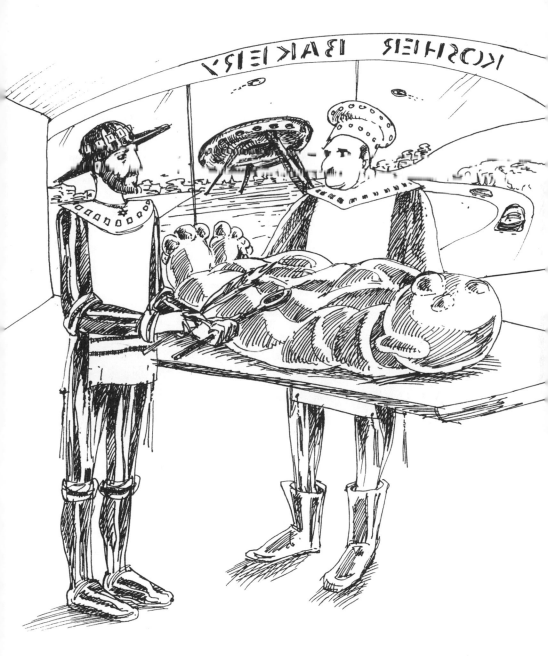

*"Back off, I'm a Rabbi"*

"The moons are all full and he's begun to sprout hair all over his face."

"It's called stubble, YENTA. It's something that happens to men without beards."

"Like excuse me, Mr. Older Type Person, did I like hear them call you like, y'know, Rabbi?" It was an athletic-looking blonde teenager. A large mallet protruded from her duffel bag along with what appeared to be fence posts. Baruch Rogers nodded. "Cool. So, like, what kind of, y'know, monster is everybody like, chasing?"

"A Golem. A soulless lump of clay in humanoid form, given a semblance of life through mystical means. Some have favored placing a piece of parchment inscribed with holy words either on the creation's forehead or in its mouth, while others have chosen to write the word *emet*, truth, on its forehead—"

"Like, in not a vampire, you're saying?"

"No," said the Rabbi, indignant over her interruption of his discourse, "not a vampire."

"Or a demon?"

"No, not a demon either. Our great sages tell us..." But she was already gone, swallowed up by the darkness.

"Young people today can be so impatient and rude," sighed Rogers.

"If she wanted a lecture, Rebbe," observed the computer, "wouldn't she be hanging out in her school library instead of running around out here?"

*Nachman Beitz came out of the rain into the un-lit lobby of the Motel Kanzoil, shrugging out of a wet yellow raincoat. "Mama! Why are you sitting here in the dark?" He flicked the light switch. Nothing happened. "Oh. I'll go get a new illuminator globe."*

*A creaky voice answered him. "No, it's all right, bubbele, I'll just sit here in the dark. You have more important things to do, like stalking some big shtarker of a monster in the rain and maybe catching your death of cold, while I sit here in the dark worrying. Too busy you are even to make a phone call to me to tell me that you're all right. Nu, tell me about this Golem that's more important than your own mother. Did he give birth to you? Did he cook and clean for you for 37 Terra years? No, don't take the time and trouble. Go, go about your important business. It's all right. I'm fine. I'll just sit here in the dark and worry."*

*"Yes, Mama. There, a brand new light globe for you." He flicked the switch again and the room was flooded in light. Nachman's mother was nowhere to be seen. He exited the lobby through the door behind the front desk. The kitchen light came on at his flick of its switch.*

*A huge figure stood in the corner by the back door holding a large stuffed bird. It had crumbled in the Golem's hands. "Anchuldig mir. I - am - sorry," mumbled the creature.*

*"Meshuggener! Psycho!" Nachman's voice had gotten shrill. "That was my dinner that I spent hours cooking!"*

Out in the storm, Rogers mused. "What could he want out there? Any ideas?"

"A—you should pardon the expression—mate perhaps?" offered YENTA.

"Impossible," said the baker. "A good husband he might make—he's a creature of yeast culture and breading—but, alas, he is seedless."

"And you accuse me of rye humor, Rebbe," said YENTA.

There was a shout from the mob. Then a scream. And then another scream. Yizkor came running towards the Rabbi and Raphael. "They've tracked him across the pet cemetery to the junkyard on the edge of the swamp. He dodged into an old groundcar, but an angry dog jumped on the hood. Somebody heard him turn on the radio to scare it off."

"That action indicates a degree of sentience that we had not previously attributed to the creature," noted YENTA. A thinking computer, he was more attuned than were humans to the possibility of sentience in non-humans.

"Com'on," said the Rabbi. "We've got to get there and destroy him. On top of everything else, he's *chometz*!"

"Wait for me," puffed Raphael. "Running a bakery is no way to get thinner. How can we destroy him?"

"You're the one with a family recipe for Golem mix and you're asking me?"

"There it is!" shouted Yizkor as the threesome dashed into the junkyard. With his twisted posture, the baker's assistant found it relatively easy to slip between the rusted-out hulls of scrapped groundcars. "Hey, this one is in better condition than what I'm driving."

The Golem stood facing the chain link fence at the perimeter of the yard. Two of his huge fingers hooked through a link as if he were about to climb. At their approach, it released its fingerhold and turned to face them. Slowly it began walking toward them.

Alarmed, the Rabbi did a quick inventory of their weaponry, Raphael carried a bread knife. Yizkor held up a butter knife. There was still butter on it. As for himself, nu, go know that a routine search for *chometz* would turn into a manhunt, or, rather, Golemhunt!

Astonishingly, the creature halted before Rogers and raised its hands in surrender. *"Ich - bin chometz. I - am - leavened. Es - iz* .... It - is - almost - Pesach."

Baruch Rogers, Space Rabbi nodded. The Golem offered no resistance as he pried the parchment from its forehead. It made some indistinct sounds and stood still, unmoving, inert in the long rain.

The last toasted crumbs of the Golem were dumped in the swamp just hours before Seder.

"I'm ruined," moaned Raphael. "I'll have to sell out to that mean green florist from downtown."

The Rabbi said nothing. He twisted his hand and shook off some loose clumps of shmutz.

*"Gevalt!"* exclaimed YENTA, "a punch card!"

The Space Rabbi pocketed it; there was, he reasoned, no sense in chancing that Raphael might try it again. Even when animated by a baker, a Goliath-sized doughboy Golem is no cream puff.

"Its end was peaceful—such peace as a soulless creature might know. Could you make out what it was trying to say to me at the end, YENTA? What it wanted?"

"Well, the first thing was 'I'm melting!' It was rather drenched and sloughing off. I can't be certain of the last thing that it said, but there's a 73.6 percent chance that it was 'If I only had a brain.'"

They turned from the Golem's final resting place and headed back toward the bakery.

"Come, Raphael," said Rabbi Rogers, "with your establishment now free of *chometz*, we may begin baking matzoh for Pesach. Community service will help you make amends for the damage that your Golem caused."

The baker's eyes lit up. "A Golem made of matzoh?" he mused.

They never saw the swamp water bubble behind them or a pulsating mass surface and slowly take on form.

## THE END — *OR IS IT?*